SHADOWS OF SHASTA.

BY

JOAQUIN MILLER,

AUTHOR OF "SONGS OF THE SIERRAS," "THE DANITES IN THE SIERRAS," ETC.

CHICAGO:

JANSEN, McCLURG & COMPANY.

1881.

TO

WHITELAW REID.

CONTENTS.

SHADOWS OF SHASTA.

INTRODUCTORY.

With vast foundations seamed and knit,
And wrought and bound by golden bars,
Sierra's peaks serenely sit
And challenge heaven's sentry-stàrs.

WHY this book? Because last year, in the heart of the Sierras, I saw women and children chained together and marched down from their cool, healthy homes to degradation and death on the Reservation. At the side of this long, chained line, urged on and kept in order by bayonets, rode a young officer, splendid in gold and brass, and newly burnished, from that now famous charity-school on the Hudson. These women and children were guilty of no crime; they were not even accused of wrong. But their fathers and brothers lay dead in battle-harness, on the mountain heights and in the lava beds; and these few silent survivors, like Israel of old, were being led into captivity—but, unlike the chosen children, never to return to the beloved heart of their mountains.

Do you doubt these statements about the treatment of the Indians? Then read this, from the man—the fiend in the form of man—who for years, and until recently, had charge of all the Indians in the United States:

> "From reports and testimony before me, I find that Indians removed to the Reservation or Indian Territory, die off so rapidly that the race must soon become extinct if they are so removed. *In this connection, I recommend the early removal of all the Indians to the Indian Territory.*"

The above coarse attempt at second-hand wit is quoted from memory. But if the exact words are not given, the substance is there; and, indeed, the idea and expression is not at all new.

I know if you contemplate the Indian from the railroad platform, as you cross the plains, you will almost conclude, from the dreadful specimens there seen, that the Indian Commissioner was not so widely out of the way in that brutal desire. But the real Indian is not there. The Special Correspondent will not find him, though he travel ten thousand miles. He is in the mountains, a free man yet; not a beggar, not a thief, but the brightest, bravest, truest man alive. Every few years, the soldiers find him; and they do not despise him when found. Think of Captain Jack, with his sixty braves, holding the whole army at bay for half a year! Think of Chief Joseph, to whose valor and virtues the brave and brilliant soldiers sent to fight him bear immortal testimony. Seamed with scars of battle, and bloody from the fight of the deadly day and the night preceding; his wife dying from a bullet; his boy lying dead at his feet; his command decimated; bullets flying thick as hail; this Indian walked right into the camp of his enemy, gun in hand, and then—not like a beaten man, not like a captive, but like a king—demanded to know the terms upon which his few remaining people could be allowed to live. When a brave man beats a brave man in battle, he likes to treat him well—as witness Grant and Lee; and so Generals Howard and Miles made fair terms with the conquered chief. The action of the Government which followed makes one sick at heart. Let us in charity call it *imbecility*. But before whose door shall we lay the dead? Months after the surrender, this brave but now heart-broken chief, cried out:

"Give my people water, or they will die. This is mud and slime that we have to drink here on this Reservation. More than half are dead already. Give us the water of our mountains. And will you not give us back just one mountain too? There are not many of us left now. We will not want much now. Give us back just one mountain, so that these women and children may live. Take all the valleys. But you cannot plow the mountains. Give us back just one little mountain, with cool, clear water, and then these children can live."

And think of Standing Bear and his people, taken by fraud and force from their lands to the Indian Territory Reservation, and after the usual hardships and wrongs incident to such removals, with no hope from a Government which neither kept its promises nor listened to their appeals, setting out to try to get back to Omaha. Think of these men, stealing away in the night, leaving their little children, their wives and parents, prostrate, dying, destitute! They were told that they could not leave—that they must stay there; that they would be followed and shot if they attempted to go away. They had no money; they had no food. They were sick and faint. They were on foot, and but poorly clad. Yet they struggled on through the snow day after day, week after week, leaving a bloody trail where they passed; leaving their dead in the snow where they passed. And this awful journey lasted for more than fifty days! And what happened to these poor Indians after that fearful journey? They did not go to the white man for help. They did not go back to their old homes. They troubled no one. They went to a neighboring friendly tribe. This tribe gave them a little land, and they instantly went to work to make homes and prepare a place for the few of their number still alive whom they had left behind. Then came the order from Washington, and the Chief was arrested while plowing in the field. In a speech made by him after the arrest, and when he was about to be taken back, the Chief said:

"I wanted to go back to my old place north. I wanted to save myself and my tribe. I built a good stable. I raised cattle and hogs and all kinds of stock. I broke land. All these things I lost by some bad man. Any one knows to take a man from a cold climate and put him in the hot sun, down in the south, it would kill him. We refused to go down there. We afterwards went down to see our friends, and see how they liked it. Brothers, I come home now. I took my brothers and friends and came back here. We went to work. I had hold of the handles of my plow. Eight days ago I was at work on my farm, which the Omahas gave me. I had sowed some spring wheat, and wished to sow some more. I was living peaceably with all men. I have never committed any crime. I was arrested and brought back as a prisoner. Does your law do that? I have been told, since the great war all men were free men, and that no man can be made a prisoner unless he does wrong. I have done no wrong, and yet I am here a prisoner. Have you a law for white men, and a different law for those who are not white?

"I have been going around for three years. I have lost all my property. My constant thought is, 'What man has done this?' Of course I know I cannot say 'no.' Whatever they say I must do, I must do it. I know you have an order to send me to the Indian Territory, and we must obey it."

Afterwards, speaking of the terrible days at the Reservation, this Indian said to an officer:

"We counted our dead for awhile, but when all my children and half the tribe were dead, we did not take any notice of anything much. When my son was dying, he begged me to take his bones back to the old home, if ever I got away. In that little box are the bones of my son; I have tried to take them back to be buried with our fathers."

I may here add, that in the meantime the brother of this Indian, who was left in charge of the tribe, was accused of trying to get away also. He protested his innocence, but the agent had him arrested and brought before him. Then he ordered him to be ironed. The proud, free savage begged not to be put in irons, but the brutal agent persisted. The Indian resisted, *and was shot dead on the spot.*

Think of the Cheyennes last year. They, too, had tried to escape from the Reservation, and reach their homes through the deep snow.

This was their only offense. No man had ever accused them of any other crime than this love of their native haunts, this longing for home. They were dying there on the Reservation; more than half had already died. And now, when taken, they refused to go back. The officer attempted to starve them into submission. They were shut up in a pen without food, naked, starving, the snow whistling through the pen, children freezing to death in their mother's arms! But they would not submit. Knowing now that they must die, they determined to die in action rather than freeze and starve, like beasts in a pen. At a concerted signal, they attempted to break through the soldiers and reach the open plain. An old man was carried on the back of his tottering son; a mounted soldier pursued them, and hacked father and son to pieces with the same sabre-cuts. A mother was seen flying over the snow with two children clinging about her neck. The wretched savages separated and ran in all directions. But the mounted men cut them down in the snow. No one asked, or even would accept, quarter. They fought with sticks, stones, fists, their teeth, like wild beasts. They wanted to die. One little group escaped to a ravine. There they were found killing each other with a sort of knife made from an old piece of hoop.

And yet you believe man-hunting is over in America!

It is impossible to write with composure or evenness on this subject. One wants to rise up and crush things.

I have mentioned two tribes near at hand, whose histories are not unfamiliar to the public ear. But what if I should recite the wrongs of tribes far away—far beyond the Rocky Mountains—where the Indian Agent has to answer to no one? You would not believe one-tenth part told you. The terrible stories of the Cheyennes and the Poncas are very mild chapters in the history of our Indian policy.

Under the stars and stripes, these scenes are repeated year after year; and they will be continued until they are made impossible by the civilization and sense of justice which righted that other though far less terrible wrong.

As that greatest man has said, "We are making history in America." This is a conspicuous fact, that no one who would be remembered in this century should forget. We are making dreadful history, dreadfully fast. How terrible it will all read when the writer and reader of these lines are long since forgotten! Ages may roll by. We may build a city over every dead tribe's bones. We may bury the last Indian deep as the eternal gulf. But these records will remain, and will rise up in testimony against us to the last day of our race.

J. M.

CHAPTER I.

MOUNT SHASTA.

To lord all Godland! lift the brow
Familiar to the moon, to top
The universal world, to prop
The hollow heavens up, to vow
Stern constancy with stars, to keep
Eternal watch while eons sleep;
To tower proudly up and touch
God's purple garment-hems that sweep
The cold blue north! Oh, this were much!

Where storm-born shadows hide and hunt
I knew thee, in thy glorious youth,
And loved thy vast face, white as truth;
I stood where thunderbolts were wont
To smite thy Titan-fashioned front,
And heard dark mountains rock and roll;
I saw the lightning's gleaming rod
Reach forth and write on heaven's scroll
The awful autograph of God!

AND what a mighty heart these Sierras have! Kissing the purple of heaven now, and now in their awful deeps hiding the shrinking form of darkness from the sun.

The shaggy monsters that prowl there, the mountains of gold that lie waiting there, the mystery and the splendor! Oh keep with me, my friend, for a little while in the Sierras; breathe their balm and health, see their sublimity, feel their might and their majesty; step upward, as on stepping stairs to heaven; and my word for it, you will be none the worse.

In a canyon here, deep, deep, away down in the darkness, where night seems to have an abiding place, where the sun sifts through the pine-tops timidly, where the loftiest trees tiptoe up and seem to strive to reach out of the edge of the chasm, there gurgles a little muddy stream among the boulders, about the miners' legs, as they bend their backs wearily and toil for gold.

Here the smoke curls up from a low log cabin; there a squirrel barks a nut on the roof of a ruined and deserted miner's home, and away up yonder, where the deep gorge is so narrow you can almost leap across it, the wild beasts prowl as if it were really night, and great owls beat their wings against the boughs of the dense wood in everlasting darkness. But high over gorge and wilderness, gleaming against the cold blue sky, towers Mount Shasta, the monarch of the Sierras.

Here, where the canyon debouches into the little valley, once stood a populous mining camp; and a little further on, where the sun fell in full splendor, a few farms of a primitive kind, tended by broken-down old miners, lay.

The old glory of the camp was gone, and only a few battered and crippled men were left. It was as if there had been a great battle of the giants, and the victorious and successful had gone away with all the fruits of victory, and left the wounded, the helpless, the half-hearted behind. The mining camp at the mouth of the great canyon had been worked out, so far as the placer mines went, and these few broken men who remained, as a rule, were turning their attention to other things. Here one had planted a little garden on the hillside, on a spot that had once been a graveyard. There, an old lawyer had grown grape-vines all over and about the door and chimney of his cabin, till men said it looked like a spider-web.

But old Forty-nine only bored deeper and deeper into the spur of the mountain, and paid but little attention to any of the changes that went on around him. He had been working in that tunnel alone for nearly twenty-five years. He was a man with a history—men said a murderer. He shunned men, and men shunned him. Was he rich? He professed to be very poor; men said he must be worth a million. Would a man work on twenty-five years in one tunnel, and all alone, for nothing? But if rich, why did he remain?

Still further down, and quite on the edge of the valley, stood another cabin. And this was quite overgrown with vines, and was quite hidden away in a growth of pines that gathered over it. Then there was an undergrowth of fruit trees that grew inside the fence and about the lonely porch. On this porch had sat, for years and years, a tawny, silent old woman. She was sickly—had neither wealth, wit nor beauty—and so, so far as the world went, was left quite alone.

But there was another and an all-sufficient reason why neither man or woman came that way. She was an Indian. Do not imagine this a wild Indian woman. Indian she was; but remember, the Catholics had more than half civilized nearly all the native Californians long before we undertook to kill them.

This Indian woman would have been called by strangers a Mexican woman. She was very religious, and had imbued her boy with all her beautiful faith and simple piety.

I know that the spectacle of an old Indian woman and her "half-breed" son, represented as the morality and religion of a camp made up of "civilized" Saxons, will seem somewhat novel to you. But I knew this Indian boy and his mother well, and know every foot of the ground I intend to go over, and every fact I propose to narrate. And if you are not prepared to receive this as truth, I prefer you to close this page right here.

To make a moment's digression, with your permission, let me state briefly and frankly, once for all, that the only really religious, unquestioning and absolutely devout Christians I ever met in America are the Indians. I know of no other people so faithful and so blindly true to their belief, outside of the peasantry of Italy. Be their beautiful faith born of ignorance or what, I do not say. I simply assert that it exists. There is no devotion so true as that of a converted Indian. Maybe it is the devotion of idolatry, the faith of superstition. But I repeat, it is sincere. And let me further say, it seems to me whatever is worth believing at all, is worth believing utterly and entirely—just as these simple children of the wilderness believe, without doubt or question.

I know nothing so beautiful—may I say picturesque?—as the Ummatilla Indians of Oregon at worship on Sunday. Not a man, woman or child of all the tribe absent. Not one voice silent when the hymns are given out, in all that vast, gaily colored and singular assemblage.

This is the tribe of which the white settlers asked and received protection last year when the Shoshonees ravaged the country, beat off the soldiers, and slew some of the settlers. And yet there is a bill before Congress to-day to take away the few remaining acres from this tribe and open up the place to white settlers. Indeed, it seems that every member of Congress from Oregon has just this one mission; for the first, and almost the only thing he does while there, is to introduce and urge the passage of this bill, whereby the red man is to be turned out of his well-tilled fields, and the white man turned into them.

In truth, these very fields have long been staked off and claimed by bold, bad white men, who hover about the borders of this Reservation, waiting for the long-promised law which is to take this land from the owners and give it to them. They nominate their members of Congress on his pledge and bond, and constant promise, to take this land from the Indian. They vote for and elect the only member of Congress from this State on that promise, certain that their absolute ownership of this graveyard of the Indian is only a question of time. Year by year the graveyard grows broader; the fields grow narrower; they grow less in number; for now and then an Indian is found wandering away from the Reservation to his former hunting-grounds and ancient graves of his fathers. He seldom comes back. Sometimes his murderers trouble themselves to throw the body in the brush or some gorge or cañyon. But most frequently it is left where it falls. To say that all the people or the best people of this brave young State approve of this, would be unfair—untrue. Yet this does not save the Indian, who is doing his best to fit into the new order of things around him. He is shot down, and neither grand or petit jury can be found to punish his murderer.

But to the story. This little piece of land where the old Indian woman had lived and brought up her boy, was rich and valuable. It was therefore coveted by the white man. At first men had said: "She will die soon; the boy will then sell the hut for a song, gamble off the money, and then go the way of all who are stained with the dark and tawny blood of the savage—death in a ditch from some unknown rifle, or death by the fever in the new Reservation." But the old woman still lived on; and the boy, by his industry, sobriety, duty and devotion to his mother, put to shame the very best among the new generation of white men in the mountains. The singular manhood of John Logan was the subject of remark by all who knew him. With the few true men on this savage edge of the world it made him fast friends; with the many outlaws and evil natures it made him the subject of envy and bitter hatred.

What power behind this boy had lifted him up and led him on? Surely no Indian woman, wholly unlettered in the ways of the white man, good and true as she may have been, had brought him up to this high place on which he now stood. Who was his father? and what strong hand had reached out all these years and kept his mother there in that little hut with her boy, while her tribe perished or passed away to the hated and horrible Reservation down toward the sea?

Who was his father? The Camp had asked this a thousand times. The boy himself had looked into the deep, pathetic eyes of his mother, and asked the question in his heart for many and many a year; but he never opened his lips to ask her. It was too sad, too sacred a subject, and he would not ask of her what she would not freely give. And now she lay dying there alone on the porch, as her boy stopped to talk with the two children, "the babes in the wood," and her secret hidden in her own heart.

And who were the "babes in the wood?" Little waifs, fugitives, hiding from the man-hunters. As a rule in early days, when the settlers killed off the adult Indians in their forays, they took the children and brought them up in slavery. But the girl—the eldest, stronger and lither of these two dark little creatures—darting, hiding, stealing about this ruined old camp, was so wild and spirited, even from the first, that no one wanted her. And then she was dangerously bright, and above all, she did not quite look the Indian; men doubted if she really were an Indian or no, sometimes. But I remember hearing old Leather-Nose, as he sat on a barrel one night in the grocery, and squirted amber at the back-log, say: "I guess, by gol, she 's Injun: She's devilish enough. She don't look the Injun, I know; but its the cussedness that makes me know she 's Injun."

"And when did she come to the camp?" asked a respectable stranger.

"Don 't know. That's it. Nobody don 't know, and nobody don 't care, I guess."

"Well, don 't you know where she came from? Children don 't come down, you know, like rain or snow. There were about fifty little children left in the Mountain-meadow massacre. They are somewhere. These may be some of them. Don't you know who brought them here, or how they came?" asked the honest stranger, leaning forward and looking into the faces of the wrinkled and hairy old miners.

An old miner turned his quid again and again, and at last feeling scant interest in the ragged little sister who led her little brother about by the hand, and stood between him and peril as she kept their liberty—drily answered, along with his fellows, as follows: "Some said an old Indian that died had her; but I don't know. Forty-nine knows most about her. When he's short of grub, and that's pretty often now, I guess, why she has to do the best she can."

"O, it was a sick looking thing at first. Why, it wasn't that high, and was all hair and bones," growled out an old gray miner, in reply to the man.

"Yes; and don't you know when we called it the 'baby,' and it used to beg around about the cabins? The poor little barefooted brat."

"Yes, and when the 'baby' nearly starved, and eat some raw turnips that made it sick."

"Yes, and got the colic—"

"Yes, and Gambler Jake got on his mule and started for the doctor."

"Yes, an' got in a poker game at Mariposa, and didn't get back for four days."

"Yes, and the doctor didn't come; and so the baby got well."

"Yes, just so, just so." And old Col. Billy bobbed his head, and fell to thinking of other days.

This little piece of land where the old Indian woman had lived so long, and about which she had built a fence, was very valuable indeed. Valley land was scarce here in the mountains; and there was a young orchard, the only thing of the kind in the country. And then the roads forked there, and two little rivers ran together there, and that meant that a town would spring up there as the country became settled, farms opened, and the Indians were swept away. Evil-minded men are never without resources. The laws are made to restrain such men; but on the border there is no law enforced. So you see how powerful are the wicked there; how powerless the weak, though never so well disposed.

In the far West, if an Indian is in your way,

you have only to report him to the Agent of the Indian Reservation. That is all you have to do. He disappears, or dies. This Indian Agent is only too anxious to fill up his wasting ranks of Indians. They are dying every day. And if they all should die, sooner or later the fact may be known at Washington, and in the course of a few years the Reservation and office would be abolished together. And then each additional Indian contributes greatly to the Agent's income, for each Indian must be fed and clothed—or at least, the Agent is permitted to draw clothing, blankets and food for every Indian brought upon the Reservation. As to the Indians receiving these things, that is quite another affair.

Well, here were men wanting this land. Down yonder, far away to the scorching South, at the edge of the level alkali lands, in a tule swamp, where the Indians taken from the mountains were penned up and dying like sheep in a corral, was a bold, enterprising Indian Agent who was gathering in, under orders of his Government, all the Indians of Northern California. He could appoint a hundred deputies, and authorize them to bring in the Indians wherever found.

The two children—"the babes in the wood"—had been taken to the Reservation; but being bold and active, they contrived to soon escape and return to the mountains. Men whispered that the girl owed her escape to the great and growing favor in which she was held by one of the deputy agents, who, with his partner, a rough and coarse-grained man, had their homes in this camp. The cabin of these two deputy agents, Dosson and Emens, stood not far from that of old Forty-Nine. But so far as I can remember, the old man and the newly appointed deputy agents had always been at enmity.

This Dosson was certainly a bad man. He was in every sense of the word a desperado, and so was his partner; just the men most wanted by the head agent at the Reservation to capture and bring in Indians.

But whether this girl owed her escape or not to this ruffian, Dosson, certain it is that on her return she avoided his cabin, and when not in the woods, hovered about that of old Forty-Nine. This enraged Dosson beyond degree. To add to his anger, she now began to show a particular preference for John Logan. The idea of having an Indian for a rival was more than this ignorant and brutal Deputy Agent could well bear, and he set to work at once to rid himself of the object of his hatred.

The hard and merciless man-hunter almost shouted with delight at a new idea which now came upon him with the light and suddeness of a revelation. He ran at once to his partner, and told him of his determination.

Then these two men sat down and talked a long time together. They made marks in the sand with sticks. They set up little stakes in the sand, and seemed delighted as they reached their heads out and looked down from the mouth of their tunnel toward the Indian farm.

That night these two men stole down together, and set up stakes and made corner marks about John Logan's land while he slept, and then rolled themselves in their blankets, and spent the night inside the limits of their new location. Having done this, and sent a notice of their pre-emption to the Surveyor General, to be filed as their declaration of claim to the little farm with the orchard, they entered complaint against John Logan, and so sat down to await results.

Meantime, this old woman sat alone, with a great dog by her side, sick and desolate, waiting her sun of life to set, piously waiting, dark browed, thoughtful; while her tall handsome boy, meek, obedient, with the awful curse of Cain upon his brow, the mark of Indian blood, was toiling on up in the canyon alone.

You had better be a negro—you had better be ten times a negro, were it possible—than be one-tenth part an Indian in the West. The Indian will have little to do with one who is part Indian. And as for the white man, unless the Indian is willing to be his slave, do him homage and service, he would sooner take a leper in his house or to his heart.

Up and above the Indian woman's house, in the dense wood and on the spur of the mountain, wound an old Indian trail. Along this trail, above the hidden house, stole two little creatures—tawny, sunburnt, ragged, wretched, yet full of affection for each other. These were the two wretched children escaped from the Reservation. They were now being harbored by old Forty-nine. For this he was liable to be arrested and punished. Knowing this, he kept his gun loaded and standing in the corner of his cabin, where the children slept at night.

How strange that this one man, the most despised and miserable, should be the only one to reach a hand to help these little waifs of the woods! And who knew or who cared from where they came? They did not look the Indian, though they acted it to perfection. They would run away and hide from the face of man. Yet the girl, under the passionate California sun, was almost blossoming into womanhood. They were called brother and sister. God knows if they were or no. Break up tribes, families, as these had been broken up—fire into a flock of young quails all day—and who knows how soon or where the few that escape may gather together again, or if they will know each other when they meet, years after in the woods?

Children are so impressionable. They had heard some one in the camp call the old Indian woman who sat forever on the porch in the dense foliage, with the big dog beside her, a witch. They did not know what that meant. But they knew it was something dreadful, and they shunned and abhorred her accordingly. Yet the girl knew John Logan, her tall handsome son, well, and liked him, too.

As they stole along the dim old Indian trail, their necks were stretched toward the old Indian woman's hut below. They were as noiseless as two panthers. At last the girl stopped, stood still, pointed and half pushed the boy before and in through the thicket, past an occasional lonely cabin, toward the widow's woody home.

This old woman had long been ailing. She was now very ill. You are surprised to learn of sickness in the heart of the Sierras? I tell you that if you were to wash down mountains and uproot forests in the moon—were such a thing possible—the ague would sieze hold of you and shake you for it. Nature is revengeful. But to return to the wilderness.

What a wilderness this was! Only here and there, at long intervals, a little cabin down in the deep, dense wood; these cabins scattered as if the hand of some mighty sower had reached out over the wilderness, and had sown and strown them there, to take root and grow to some great harvest of civilization. The narrow Indian trail wound along, almost entirely hidden by overhanging woods—a trail that turned and twisted at every little obstacle; here it was the prostrate form of some patriarch tree, or here it curved and cork-screwed in and out through mighty forest-kings, that stood like comrades in ranks of battle.

Where did this little Indian trail lead to? Where did it begin? How many a love-tale had been told in the shadow of those mighty trees that reached their long, strong arms out over the heads of all passers-by, in a sort of priestly benediction?

Where did the Indian trail lead to? To the West. But leaves were strewn thick along it now. The Indian had gone, to come back no more. Ever to the West points the Indian's path. Ever down to the great gold shore of the vast west sea leads the Indian's path. And there the waves sweep in and obliterate his foot-prints forever.

The two half-wild children who had disappeared down the dim trail a few moments before, now suddenly re-appear. They are eager and excited. This boy cannot be above ten years old; yet he looks old as a man. The girl may be twelve, fifteen, or even sixteen. Age at such a period is a matter of either blood or climate. She has a shock of unkempt hair; she wears a tattered dress of as many colors as Jacob's coat. She has one toeless boot on one foot; on the other she wears a shoe so big that it might hold both her feet. Down over this shoe rolls a large red woolen stocking, leaving her shapely little ankle bleeding from brier-scratches. In her hand she swings a large, coarse straw hat by its broad red ribbons. Her every limb is full of force and fire; her voice is firm and resolute, but not rapid. Hers is a splendid energy, needing but proper direction.

Her brother, who puffs and pants at her side, is named Johnny; but the wild West, which has a habit of naming things because they look it, has dubbed him "Stumps," since he is short and fat. He is half-clad in a pair of tattered pants, a great straw hat, and a full, stuffy, check shirt, which is held in subjection by a pair of hand-made woolen suspenders—the work of his sister.

Both are out of breath—both are looking back wildly; but Stumps huddles up again and again close under his sister's arm, as if he fears he might be followed, and looks to her for protection. She draws him close to her, and then looking back, and then down into his upturned face, says breathlessly:

"Stumps! Oh, Stumps, did you get 'em, Stumps?"

The boy shrinks closer to his sister, and again looking back, and then seeing for a certainty that he is not followed, he grows bolder and says:

"Git 'em, Carats? Look there! And that 'un is your'n, Carats; and you can have both of 'em if you want 'em, for I don't feel hungry now, Carats," and here he hitches up his pants, and wipes his nose on his sleeve.

"Why, Stumps, don't you feel hungry now?" Then suddenly beholding two upheld ruddy peaches, she catches her breath, and says: "Oh, oh!" and she starts back and throws up her hands. "Oh, the pretty, pretty peaches!"

"Here, take 'em both, Carrie—I ain't hungry now."

"No, I don't want but one, Stumps—one 's enough. Why, how you tore your pants; and your shin 's a bleeding, too. Why, poor Stumps!"

Stumps, looking back, cries:

"Shoo! Thar war a dog—yes, thar war a dog! And what do you think! Shoo! I thought I heard somethin' a comin'. Carats, old Miss Logan, the Injun woman, seed me!"

"Why, Stumps! No?"

"Yes, she did. When I clim' the fence, and slid down that sapling in the yard, there she laid on the porch on her shuck-bed a-shaking with the ager. And, Carats, she was a-looking right straight at me—yes, she was; so help me, she was."

"Why, Stumps; and what did she do! Didn't she holler, and say 'Seek 'em, Bose?' "

"Carats, she didn't; and that's what 's the matter—and that 's why I don't want to eat any peaches, Carats. Carats, I wish she had—I do, I do, so help me. Let 's not eat 'em—let 's take 'em back—Carrie, sister Carrie, let 's take 'em back."

Carrie thoughtfully and tenderly gazes in his face.

" Let 's take 'em to old Forty-nine, Johnny. There ain't nothing he can eat, you know; an' then he's been a-shakin' since melon-time, —an' Johnny, I don't think we are very good to him, anyhow."

Stumps, scratching his bleeding shin with his foot, exclaims:

" I've barked my shin, and I've tore'd my pants, an' I don't care! But I won't take him a peach that I've stoled. Why, what would he think, Carats? He'd die dead, he would, if he thought I'd stoled them peaches from the poor old sick Injun woman; yes he would, Carats."

" Johnny, I'll tell him we found 'em," as Stumps looks doubtingly at her, " tell him we found 'em in a tree, Stumps. Yes tell him we found 'em away up in the top of a cedar tree."

" But I don't want to tell no lie, nor do nothin' bad no more, and I want to go home, I do."

" Well, Stumps—Johnny, brother Johnny, what will we do with them? We can't stand here all day. I want to go home, too. Oh, this hateful, hateful peach! I want to go right off!" and the girl, hiding her face in her hands, begins to weep.

"Oh, sister Carrie—sister, don't, don't; sister, don't, don't!"

"Then let's eat 'em."

"I don't like peaches."

"I don't like peaches either!" cries Carrie, throwing back her hair, wiping her eyes, and trying to be bright and cheerful. "I never could eat peaches. I like pine-nuts, and cow-cumbers, and tomatuses, and—pine-nuts. Oh, I'm very fond of pine-nuts. I like pine-nuts roasted, and tomatuses, an' I like chestnuts raw, an' tomatuses. Don't you like pine-nuts and tomatuses, Johnny, and cow-cumbers?"

"I don't like nothin' any more."

"Then, Johnny, take 'em back."

"I—I—I take 'em back by myself? I take 'em back, an' hear old Bose growl, and look into her holler eyes?" Here the boy shudders, and looking around timidly, he creeps closer to his sister and says, as he again gazes back in the direction of the Indian woman's cabin: "I'd be afraid she might be dead, Car-ats, an' there'd be nobody to hold the dog.

Oh, I see her holler eyes looking at me all the time. If she'd only let the dog come. Confound her! If she'd only let the dog come!"

"Oh, Johnny, Johnny—brother Johnny, come, lets go home! Shoo! There 's somebody coming. It 's John Logan, coming home from his work."

As the girl speaks, John Logan, the sick woman's son, a strong handsome man, only brown as if browned by the sun, with a pick on his shoulder and a gold-pan slanting under his arm, comes whistling along the trail. Seeing the children, he stops and says:

"Why, children, good evening! What are you running away for? Come, come now, don't be so shy, my little neighbors, and don't give the trail all to me because I happen to be a man, and the strongest. Come, Johnny, give me your hand. There! an honest, chubby little fist it is. Why, what have you got in your other hand? Been gathering nuts, hey? You little squirrel! Give me a nut, won't you."

Carrie approaches, dives her hand into her ragged pocket and reaches the man a heaped handful of nuts.

"There, if you'll have nuts I'll bring you nuts; I'll bring you lots of nuts, I will; I'll bring you a bushel of nuts, an'—some tomatuses."

"Oh, you are too kind. But now I must hasten home to mother. Come, shake hands again, and say good-bye." The girl gives her left hand. "No your right hand."

Carrie is bothered, and slips the peach in her left hand behind, and, with a lifted face, full of glow and enthusiasm, says:

"I'll bring you a whole bag full of nuts, I will," and she reaches him her hand eagerly.

"Oh Carrie, I have a nice little surprise for you, and if you won't tell I'll let you into the secret. You won't tell?"

He comes close to her, sits down his gold-pan, and resting his pick on the ground, with his two hands on the top of the handle, leans toward her and looks into her innocent uplifted face.

The girl's eyes brighten, and she seems to grow tall and beautiful under his earnest gaze.

"I won't tell, sir. Oh, please to trust me, sir—I won't tell, Mr. John Logan!"

The boy eagerly comes forward also.

"I won't tell, neither. I won't tell neither; so help me!"

"Well, then, come close to me, Johnny, come close up here, and look in my face—there! Why, I declare the pleasure I now have, telling you this, is more than gold! And I need money sadly enough."

"You're awful poor, ain't you?" asked Stumps, hitching up his pants.

"Been workin' all day and ain't got much in the pan," says Carrie, looking sidewise at the few colors of gold in the bottom edge of the pan.

"Ah, yes, Carrie. Look at my hands—hard and rough as the bark of a tree; but I don't mind that, Carrie, I was born here, I was born poor, I shall live poor and die poor. But I don't mind it, Carrie. I have my mother to love and look after, and while she lives I am content."

The girl looks at the woods, looks at the man, and then once more at the woods, and at last in her helplessness to solve the problem, falls to eating nuts, as usual; while the man continues, as if talking to himself:

"This is the peace of Paradise; and see the

burning bush! Now I can well understand that Moses saw the face of God in the bush of fire."

"Oh," the girl says to herself, "if he only would be cross! If he only would say something rough to us! If he only would cuss."

She resolves to say or do something to break the spell. She asks eagerly:

"Are you going to give something to Stumps and me?—I mean Johnny and me?"

"Yes, yes, to-morrow evening, after my work is done. And now I am going to tell you and Johnny what it is. It ain't much; it's the least little thing in the world; but I don't deserve any credit for even that—it's my poor dear old mother's idea. She has laid there, day after day, on the porch, and she has been thinking, not all the time of her own sickness and sorrow, but of others, as well; and she has thought much of you."

The boy stands far aside, and at mention of this he jerks himself into a knot, his head drops down between his shoulders, his mouth puckers up, and he exclaims "Oh, hoka!"

"Thought of me?" says Carrie.

"Of you, Carrie. And listen; I must tell

you a little story. When I was a very young man, and killed my first grizzly bear, I bought a little peach-tree and planted it in the corner of the yard, as people sometimes plant trees to remember things. Well, my mother, she had the ague that day powerful, for it was after melon-time, and she sat on the porch and shook, and shook, and shook, and watched me plant it, and when I got done, my mother she cried. I don't know why she cried, Carrie, but she did. She cried and she cried, and when I went up to her, and put my arms around her neck and kissed her, she only cried the more, for she was sort of hysteric-like, you know, and she said she knew she'd never live to eat any fruit off of that tree."

Carrie stops eating nuts a moment.

"But she will—she will get well, Mr. John Logan—she will get well, won't she?"

"Ah, indeed, I believe she will get well, but whether she ever gets right well or not, she certainly will live to eat peaches from that tree. Carrie, we've talked it all over, and what do you think? Why, now listen, I will tell you. This tree that I planted, and that my poor sick mother was afraid she would not live to eat the fruit from—this tree was a peach tree."

Carrie again takes out a handful of nuts from her pocket, as if she would like to eat them. She looks at them a second, throws them away, and hastens to one side.

"I want to go home," cries Stumps. "I don't like peaches, Mr. John Logan. I don't —I don't—so help me," and the boy jerks at his pants wildly.

John Logan turns to him kindly. "Why, you never had a peach in your little hand in your life." Then turning to Carrie: "Yes, Carrie, there has grown this year, high up in the sun on that tree, side by side, two—and only two—red, ripe peaches. Why, children, don't run away! Wait one moment, and I will go a little way with you. As I was about to say, these two peaches are at last ripe. I own I was the least bit afraid, even after I saw them there on that bough one Summer morning, that even then my mother might die before they became fully ripe. But now they are ripe, and this evening I shall pull them. And to-morrow, after my day's work is done, my sick mother shall eat one, and you two shall eat the other."

Carrie puts up her hand and backs away.

"Don't—don't—don't call me Carrie; call me Carats—Carats—Carats—like the others do!"

'Why, Carrie! What in the world is the matter with you?"

"If a body steals, Mr. John Logan—if a body steals—what had a body better do?"

"Why, the Preacher says a body should confess—confess it, feel sorry, and be forgiven."

"I can't—I can't confess, and I can't be forgiven!"

John Logan starts!

"You—you, Carrie; is it you? Then you have already confessed, and He will forgive you!"

"But such stealing as this nobody—nothing—can forgive," falling on her knees. "I—I made my little brother steal your peaches!"

"You!—you made him steal my two peaches that I wanted for my sick mother? You—*you*, Carrie?"

Stumps rushed forward

"No—No! I done it myself! I done it all myself—I did, so help me!"

"But I made him do it!" cries Carrie. "I am the biggest, and I knew better—I knew better. But we could n't eat 'em. Here they are—oh I am so glad we couldn't eat 'em!" And they fall on their knees at his feet together; four little hands reach out the peaches to him eagerly, earnestly, as if in prayer to Heaven.

The man takes their little hands, and, choking with tears, says, in a voice full of pathos and pity, and uncovering his head, with lifted face, as he remembers something of the story the good Priest so often read to his mother: "and there was more joy in Heaven over the one that was found, than over the ninety-and-nine that went not astray."

CHAPTER II.

TWENTY CARATS FINE.

A land that man has newly trod,
A land that only God has known,
Through all the soundless cycles flown.
Yet perfect blossoms bless the sod,
And perfect birds illume the trees,
And perfect unheard harmonies
Pour out eternally to God.

A thousand miles of mighty wood
Where thunder-storms stride fire-shod;
A thousand flowers every rod,
A stately tree on every rood;
Ten thousand leaves on every tree,
And each a miracle to me;
And yet there be men who question God!

At just what time these two waifs of the woods appeared in camp even Forty-nine could not tell. They were first seen with the Indian woman who went about among the miners, picking up bread and bits of coin by dancing, singing and telling fortunes. These two Indian women were great liars, and rogues altogether. I need not add that they were partly civilized.

The little girl had been taught to dance and sing, and was quite a source of revenue to the two Indian women, who had perhaps bought or stolen the children. As for the boy—poor stunted, starved little thing—he hung on to his sister's tattered dress all the time with his little red hand, wherever she went and whatever she did. He was her shadow; and he was at that time little more than a shadow in any way.

Sometimes men pitied the little girl, and gave very liberally. They tried to find out something about her past life; for although she was quite the color of the Indian, she had regular features, and at times her poor pinched face was positively beautiful. The two children looked as if they had been literally stunted in their growth from starvation and hardship.

Once a good-hearted old miner had bribed the squaws to let the children come to his cabin and get something to eat. They came, and while they were gorging themselves, the boy sitting close up to the girl all the time, and looking about and back over his shoulder and holding on to her dress, this man questioned her about her life and history. She did not like to talk; indeed, she talked with difficulty at first, and her few English words fell from her lips in broken bits and in strange confusion. But at length she began to speak more clearly as she proceeded with her story, and became excited in its narration. Then she would stop and seem to forget it all. Then she went on, as if she was telling a dream. Then there would be another long pause, and confusion, and she would stammer on in the most wild and incoherent fashion, till the old miner became quite impatient, and thought her as big an imposter as the Indian woman whom she called her mother. He finally gave them each a loaf of bread, and told them they could go back to their lodge. This lodge consisted of a few poles set up in wigwam fashion, and covered with skins and old blankets and birch. A foul, ugly place it was, but in this wigwam lived two Indian women and these two children.

Men, or rather beasts—no, beasts are decent creatures; well then, monsters, full of bad rum, would prowl about this wretched lodge at night, and their howls, mixed with those of the savages, whom they had made also drunk, kept up a state of things frightful to think of in connection with these two sensitive, starving little waifs of the woods.

Who were they, and where did they come from? Sometimes these children would start up and fly from the lodge at night, and hide away in the brush like hunted things, and only steal back at morning when all was still. At such times the girl would wrap her little brother (if he was her brother) in her own scant rags, and hold him in her arms as he slept.

One night, while some strange Indians were lodging there, a still more terrible scene transpired in this dreadful little den than had yet been conceived. The two children fled as usual into the darkness, back into the deep woods. Shots were heard, and then a death-yell that echoed far up and down the canyon. Then there were cries, shrieks of women, as if they were being seized and borne away. Fainter and fainter grew their cries; further and further, down on the high ledge of the canyon in the darkness, into the deep wood, they seemed to be borne. And at last their cries died away altogether.

The next morning a dead Indian was found at the door of the empty lodge. But the women and the children were nowhere to be seen. Some said the Indian Agent's men had come to take the Indians away, and that the man resisting had been shot, while the women and children were taken to the Reservation, where they belonged. But there was a darker story, and told under the breath, and not spoken loud. Let it be told under the breath, and briefly here, also. Some drunken wretches had shot the Indians, carried the women down to the dark woods above the deep swollen river, and then, after the most awful orgies ever chronicled, murdered them and sunk their bodies in the muddy river.

It was nearly a week after that the two children stole down from the wooded hill-side into the trail, where old Forty-nine found them on his return from work. They were so weak they could not speak or cry out for help. They could only reach their little hands and implore help, as, timid and frightened, they tottered towards this first human being they had dared to face for a whole week.

The strong man hesitated a moment; they looked so frightful he wanted to escape from their presence. But his grand, noble nature came to the surface in a second; and dropping his pick and pan in the trail, he caught up the two children, and in a moment more was, with one in each arm, rushing down the trail to his cabin. He met some men, and passed others. They all looked at him with wonder. One even laughed at him.

And it is hard to comprehend this. There were good men—good in a measure; men who would have gallantly died to save a woman—men who were true men on points of honor; yet men who could not think of even being civil to an Indian, or any one with a bit of Indian blood in his veins. Is our government responsible for this? I do not say so. I only know that it exists; a hatred, a prejudice, more deeply seated and unreasonable than ever was that of the old slave-dealer for the black man.

Forty-nine did not return to his tunnel the next day, nor yet the next. This cabin, wretched as it became in after years when he had fallen into evil habits, had then plenty to eat, and there the starved little beings ate as they had never eaten before.

At first the little boy would steal and hide away bread while he ate at the table. The first night, after eating all he could, he slept with both his pockets full and a chunk up his sleeve besides.

This boy was never a favorite. He was so weak, so dependent on his sister. It seemed as if he had been at one time frightened almost to death, and had never quite gotten over it. And so Forty-nine took most kindly to the girl, and they were soon fast friends. Yet ever and always her shadow, the little boy, whom Forty-nine named Johnny, kept at her side—as I have said before; his little red hand reached out and clutching at her tattered dress.

After a few weeks the girl began to tell strange, wild stories to the old man. But observing that Forty-nine doubted these, as the other man had, she called them dreams, and so would tell him these wild and terrible dreams of the desert, of blood, of murder and massacre, till the old man himself, as the girl shrank up to him in terror, became almost frightened. He did not like to hear these dreams, and she soon learned not to repeat them.

One evening a passing miner stopped, placed a broad hand on either door-jamb, and putting his great head in at the open door, asked how the little "copper-colored pets" got on.

"Pard," answered Forty-nine, kindly, and with a nod of the head back toward the children playing in the corner, "they are not coppers; no, they are not. I tell you that girl is not copper, but gold. Yes she is, Pard; she is twenty carats.

"Twenty carats gold! Well, Twenty Carats, come here! Come here, Carats," called out the big head at the door.

The girl came forward, and a big hand fell down from the door-jamb on her bushy head of hair, and the man was pleased as he looked down into the uplifted face. And so he called her "Carats," and that became her name.

Other passing miners stopped to look in at the open door where the big head had looked and talked to the timid girl, and misunderstanding the name, they called her Carrie; and Carrie she was called ever afterwards.

But the boy who had been so thin, soon grew so fat and chubby that some one named him "Stumps." There was no good trying to get rid of that name. He looked as though his name ought to be Stumps, and Stumps it was, in spite of the persistent efforts of old Forty-nine to keep the name in use which he had given him. And this was all that Forty-nine or any one could tell of these two children.

And now, how beautiful Carrie had grown by the time the leaves turned brown! Often Dosson saw her hovering about the cabin of old Forty-nine, flitting through the woods with her brother, or walking leisurely with Logan on the hill down the dim old Indian trail.

Mother Nature has her golden wedding once a year, and all the world is invited. She has many gala days, too, besides, and she celebrates them with songs and dances of delight. In the full bosomed, teeming, jocund Spring, I have seen the trees lean together and rustle their leaves in whisperings of love. I have seen them reach their long strong arms to each other, and intertwine them as if in fond affection, as the bland, warm winds, coming up from the South, blew over them and warmed their hearts of oak—old trees, too, gnarled and knotted—old fellows that had bobbed their heads together through many and many a Spring; that had leaned their lofty and storm-stained tops together through many and many a Winter; that had stood, like mighty soldiers, shoulder to shoulder, in friendships knit through many centuries. The birds sing and flutter, fly in and out of the dark deep canopies of green, build nests, and make love in myriads. How the squirrels run and chatter and frisk, and fly from branch to branch, with their bushy tails tossing in the warm wind! Under foot, ten thousand tall strange flowers and weeds and long spindled grasses grow, and reach up and up, as if to try to touch the sunlight above the tops of the oak and ash and pine and fir and cedar and maple and cherry and sycamore and spruce and tamarack, and all these that grow in common confusion here and shut out the sun from the earth as perfectly as if all things dwelt forever in cloudland.

The cabin of old Forty-nine was very modest; it hid away in the canyon as if it did not wish to be seen at all. And it was right; for verily it was scarcely presentable. It was an old cabin, too, almost as old as little "Carats," if indeed any one could tell how old she was. But it, unlike herself, seemed to be growing tired and weary of the world. She had been growing up as it had been growing down. The moss was gathering all over the round, rough logs on the outside, and the weeds and wild vines each year grew still more ambitious to get quite to the top of the cabin, and peep down into the mysterious crater of a chimney that forever smoked in a mournful and monotonous sort of way, as if watchers were there—Vestal virgins, who dared not let their fires perish, on penalty of death.

"Drunken, wretched, cracked and crazy old Forty-nine," the camp said, "he can never build a new cabin, for he can't stay sober long enough to cut down a tree." And the camp told the ugly truth.

"Why don't Forty-nine build a new cabin?" asked Gar Dosson one day, as he passed that

way, with a string of fish in his hand and a coon on his back.

"Poor dear Forty-nine 's got the shakes so he can't get time. It takes him all the time to shake, and it takes all his money to buy his ager medicine. Poor dear old Forty-nine!" and the girl seemed to get a cinder or something in her eye. * * * * *

As the sun settled low, one afternoon, and cast long, creeping shadows over the flowery land—shadows that lay upon and crept along the ground, as if they were weary of the day, and would like to lie there and sleep, and sleep, forever—the stealthy step of a man was heard approaching the old cabin. There was something of the tiger in the man's movements, and it was clear that his mission, whatever it was, was not a mission of peace. * * *

The man stands out in the clearing of the land before the cabin, and peers right and left up the trail and down the trail, and then leans and listens. Then he takes a glance back over his shoulder at his companion and follower, Gar Dosson, and being sure that he too is on the alert and close on his heels, he steps forward. Again the man leans and listens, but seeing no signs of life and hearing no sound, he straightens up, walks close to the cabin, and calls out:

"Hello, the house!" at the same time he looks to the priming of his gun, and then fixes his eye on the door as it slowly opens. He drops the breech hastily to the ground as the face of Carrie peers forth.

"Beg pardon, Carrie, my girl! Is it only you miss? Beg pardon—but we are lookin' for a gentleman—a young gentleman, John Logan."

The man is terribly embarrassed as the girl looks him straight in the face, and his companion falls back into the woods until almost hidden from view.

"Well, and why do you come here, skulking like Indians?"

The man falls back; but recovering, he says, over his shoulder, as he turns to go:

"Yes, skulking around your cabin, like that other Injun, John Logan!"

The man jerks the coon-skin cap up on his left ear as he says this, and, tossing his head, steps back into the thick woods and is gone.

Later in the evening, John Logan, gun in

hand, passes slowly and dreamily down the trail, close to old Forty-nine's cabin. Stumps and Carrie are at play in the wood close at hand, and come forth at a bound.

"Booh!" cries Carrie, darting around from behind a tree. "Booh! Mr. John Logan," continues the girl, and then with her two dimpled brown hands she throws back the glorious storm of black abundant hair, that all the time tumbles about her beautiful face.

"Why, Carrie, is that you? and Stumps, too? I am glad to see you. I—I was feeling awful lonesome."

"Been down to Squire Fields' again, have n't you?"

The girl has reached one hand out against a tree, and half leaning on it swings her right foot to and fro. John Logan starts just a little, looks at her, sighs, sets the breech of his gun on the ground, and as his eyes turn to hers, she sees he is very sad.

"Yes, Carrie, I—I am lonesome at my cabin since—since mother died. All the time, Carrie, I see her as I saw her that night, when I got home, sitting there on the porch, looking

straight out at the gate, waiting for me, her hand on the dog's head, as if to hold him."

As he says this, poor little Stumps stands up close against a tree, draws his head down, and pulls up his shoulders.

"Yes, her long bony fingers resting on his head, holding him—and the faithful dog never moving for fear he would disturb her—for she was dead."

"Oh, Mr. John Logan, don't tell me about it—don't!" and the girl's apron is again raised to her face as she shudders.

"Poor old woman with the holler eyes," says Stumps to himself, in a tone that is scarcely audible.

"But there, never mind." The strong, handsome fellow brushes a tear aside, and taking up his gun again, tries to be cheerful, and shake off the care that encompasses him.

"And you got lonesome, and went down to see Sylvia Fields, didn't you?"

Again the girl's foot swings, and she looks askance from under her dark, heavy hair, at John Logan.

"Carrie, listen to me. Ever since I can remember, my mother waited and watched for my coming at my cabin door. But now, only think how lonely it is to live there. I can't go away. I have no fortune, no friends, no people. What would people say to me and of me out in the great world? Well, I went to Squire Fields, and I had a long talk with Sylvia."

The girl starts, and almost chokes.

"Been to see Sylvia Fields!" and with her booted foot she kicks the bark of a tree with all her might. "Had a long talk with her!" Then she whirls around, plunges her hand in her pocket, and swings her dress and says, as she pouts out her mouth,

"Oh, I feel just awful!"

John Logan approaches her.

"Why, Carrie, what 's the matter?"

Carrie still swings herself, and turns her back to the man as she says, half savagely,

"I don't know what 's the matter, and I don't care what's the matter; but I feel just awful, I do! I feel just like the dickens!"

"But, Carrie, you ought to be very, very happy, with all this beautiful scenery, and the sweet air in your hair and on your rosy face. And then what a lady you have grown to be!

Now don't look cross at me like that! You ought to be as happy as a bird."

"But I ain't happy; I ain't happy a bit, I ain't!" Then, after a pause she continues:

"I don't like that Gar Dosson. He was here looking for you."

"Here? Looking for me?"

"Yes, and he called old Forty-nine Old Blossom-nose. I just hate him."

"Oh, well, Carrie, you know Forty-nine does drink dreadfully, and you know he has got a dreadful red face."

"Mr. John Logan," cries Carrie, hotly, "Forty-nine don't drink dreadfully. He don't drink dreadfully at all. He does take something for his ager, but he don't drink."

"Well, his face is dreadful red, anyway," answers John Logan.

Carrie, swinging her foot and thoughtfully looking up at the trees, says, after a pause:

"Do the trees drink? Do the trees and the bushes drink, John Logan? Their faces get awfully red in the fall, too."

"Carrie, you are cross to-day."

Carrie, shrugging her shoulders and shaking her dress as if she would shake it off her, snaps: "I ain't cross."

"Yes, you are," and the tawny man comes up to her and speaks in a kindly tone: "But come. Many a pleasant walk we have had in these woods together, and many a pleasant time we will have together still."

"We won't!"

"Ah, but we will! Come, you must not be so cross!"

The girl leans her forehead against the tree on her lifted arm, and swings her other foot. She looks down at the rounded ankle, and says, almost savagely, to herself; "She's got bigger feet than I have. She's got nearly twice as big feet, she has."

John Logan looks at the girl with a profound tenderness, as she stands there, pouting and swinging her foot. He attempts to approach her, but she still holds her brow bowed to the tree upon her arm, and seems not to see him. He shoulders his gun and walks past her, and says, kindly,

"Good-bye, Carrie."

But the girl's eyes are following him, although she would not be willing to admit it, even to herself. As he is about to disappear, she thrusts her hand madly through her hair, and pulls it down all in a heap. Still looking at him under her brows, still swinging her foot wildly, she says:

"Do you think red hair is so awful ugly?"

And what a wondrous glory of hair it was! It was so intensely black; and then it had that singular fringe of fire, or touch of Titian color, which seen in the sunset made it almost red.

The man stops, turns, comes back a step or two, as she continues:

"I do—I do! Oh, I wish to Moses I had tow hair, I do, like Sylvia Fields."

The man is standing close beside her now. He is looking down into her face and she feels his presence. The foot does not swing so violently now, and the girl has cautiously, and, as she believes, unseen, lifted the edge of her tattered sleeve to her eyes. "Why Carrie, your hair is not red." And he speaks very tenderly. "Carrie, you are going to be beautiful. You are beautiful now. You are very beautiful!"

Carrie is not so angry now. The foot stops altogether, and she lifts her face and says:

"No I ain't—I ain't beautiful! Don't you try to humbug me. I am ugly, and I know it! For, last winter, when I went down to the grocery to fetch Forty-nine—he'd gone down there to get medicine for his ager, Mr. John Logan—I heard a man say, 'She is ugly as a mud fence.' Oh, I went for him! I made the fur fly! But that did n't make me pretty. I was ugly all the same. No, I'm not pretty —I'm ugly, and I know it!"

"Oh, no, you're not. You are beautiful, and getting lovelier every day." Carrie softens and approaches him.

"Am I, John Logan? And you really don't think red hair is the ugliest thing in the world?"

"Do I really not think red hair is the ugliest thing in the world? Why, Carrie?"

Carrie, starting back, looks in his face and says, bitterly: "You do. You do think red hair is the ugliest thing in all this born world, and I just dare you to deny it. Sylvia Fields —she's got white hair, she has, and you like white hair, you do. I despise her; I despise her so much that I almost choke."

"Why, now, Carrie, what makes you despise Sylvia Fields?"

"I don't know; I don't know why I despise her, but I do. I despise her with all my might and soul and body. And I tell you, Mr. John Logan, that"—here the lips begin to quiver, and she is about to burst into tears —"I tell you, Mr. John Logan, that I do hope she likes ripe bananas; and I do hope that if she does like ripe bananas, that when bananas come to camp this fall, that she will take a ripe banana and try for to suck it; and I do hope she will suck a ripe banana down her throat, and get choked to death on it, I do."

"Oh, Carrie, this is very wicked!" cries John Logan, reproachfully, "and I must leave you if you talk that way. Good-bye," and the man shoulders his gun and again turns away.

"Well, do you think red hair is the ugliest thing in the world? Do you? Do you now?"

"Carrie, don't you know I love the beautiful, red woods of autumn?"

It is the May-day of the maiden's life; the May shower is over again, and the girl lifts her beautiful face, and says lightly, almost laughing through her tears,

"And, oh, you did like the red bush, didn't you, Mr. John Logan? And, oh, you did say that Moses saw the face of God in the burning bush, didn't you, Mr. John Logan?"

"I want you to tell me a story, I do," interposes Stumps. The boy had stood there a long time, first on one foot, then on the other, swinging his squirrel, pouting out his mouth, and waiting.

"Yes, tell us a story," urges Carrie.

"Oh, yes, tell us a story about a coon—no, about a panther—no, a bear. Oh, yes, about a bear! about a bear!" cries the boy, "about a bear!"

"Poor, half-wild children!" sighs John Logan. "Nothing to divert them, their little minds go out, curiously seeking something new and strange, just, I fancy as older and abler people's do in larger ways. Yes, I will tell you a story about a bear. And let us sit down; my long walk has tired my legs;" and he looks about for a resting place.

"Oh, here, this mossy log!" cries Stumps; "it's as soft as silk. You will sit there, and I here, and sister there."

John Logan leans his gun against a tree, hanging his pouch on the gun.

"Yes, I will sit here—and you, Carrie?"

"Here. Oh, John Logan, I just fit in."

One of Logan's arms falls loosely around Carrie, the other more loosely around Stumps.

"Yes, it's a nice fit, Carrie—could n't be better if cut out by a tailor."

Carrie, swinging her feet, and looking in his face, very happy, exclaims:

"Oh, John Logan! Don't hold me too tight—you might hurt me!"

Stumps laughs. "He don't hold me tight enough to hurt me a bit." Then looking up in his face, says, "I want a bear story, I do."

"Well, I will tell you a story out of the Bible. Once upon a time there was a great, good man—a very good and a very earnest man. Well, this very good old man, who was very bald headed, took a walk one evening; and the very good old man passed by a lot of very bad boys. And these very bad boys saw the very bald head of the very good man and they said, 'Go up, old bald head! Go up, old bald head!' And it made this good man very mad; and he turned, and he called a she-bear out of the woods, and she ate up about forty."

"Oh!" cries Stumps, aghast.

"Oh!" adds Carrie. "And he was n't a very good man. He might have been a very bald-headed man, but he was n't a very good man to have her eat all the children, Mr. John Logan."

Stumps, nursing his squirrel, with his head on one side, says:

"Well, I don't believe it, no how—I don't! What was his name—the old, bald-head?"

"His name was Elijah, sir."

"Elijah! The bald-headed Elijah! Oh, I do believe it, then; for I know when Forty-nine and the curly-headed grocery-keeper were playing poker, at ten cents ante and pass the buck—when Forty-nine went down to get his ager medicine, sister—Forty-nine, he went a blind; and the curly-headed grocery-keeper he straddled it, and then Forty-nine seed him, he did. And so help me! he raked in the pot on a Jack full. And then the curly-headed grocery-keeper jumped up, and struck his fist on the table, and he said, 'By the bald-headed Elijah!'"

Carrie nestles closer, and in a half whisper, mutters,

"I believe I'm getting a little chilly."

Stumps hears this, and says,

"Why, Carrie, I'm just a sweatin', and—"

"Shoo! What noise was that? There is some one stealing through the bush!"

John Logan, as he spoke, rose up softly and cautiously, and half bent forward as he put the two children aside and reached his gun. He looked at the cap, ran an eye along the barrel, and then twisted his belt about so that a pistol was just visible beneath his coat. The man had had an intimation of trouble. Indeed, his gun had been at hand all this time, but he did not care to frighten the two happy waifs of the woods with any thought of what might happen to him, and even to them.

These children had but one thing to dread. There was but one terrible word to them in the language. It was not hunger, not starvation,—no, not even death. It was the *Reservation!* That one word meant to them, as it means to all who are liable to be carried there, captivity, slavery, degradation, and finally death, in its most dreadful form.

And why should it be so dreaded? Make the case your own, if you are a lover of liberty, and you can understand.

Statistics show that more than three-fourths of all Indians removed to Reservations of late years, die before becoming accustomed to the new order of things.

Yet Indians do not really fear death. But they do dread captivity. They are so fond of their roving life, their vast liberty—room! An Indian is too brave to commit suicide, save in the most rare and desperate cases. But his heart breaks from home-sickness, and he dies there in despair. And then to see his helpless little children die, one by one, with the burning fever, which always overtakes the poor captives!

"How many of us died? I do not know. We counted them at first. But when there were dead women and children in every house and not men enough to bury them, I did not count any more," said one of the survivors when questioned.

In earlier times, some of these Reservations were well chosen—the one on the Ummatilla, Oregon, for example. But of late years it would seem as if the most deadly locations had been selected. Perhaps this is thought best by those in authority, as the land is soon wanted by the whites if it is at all fit for their use. And the Indians in such cases are sooner or later made to move on.

This particular Reservation in California, however, never has been and never will be required or used by any man, except for a grave.

Why, in the name of humanity, such things are left to the choice and discretion of strangers, new men, men who know nothing about Indians and care nothing for them, except so far as they can coin their blood, is incomprehensible. It is a crime. Way out yonder, in the heart of a burning plain, by the side of an alkali lake that fairly reeked with malaria, where even reptiles died, where wild fowl never were found; a place that even beasts knew better than to frequent, without wood or water, save stunted sage and juniper and slimy alkali, in the very valley of death—this Reservation had been established.

"Ah, just the place. A place where we can use our cavalry when they attempt to escape," said the young sprig of an officer, when some men with a spark of humanity dared to protest.

And that was the reason for removing it so far from the sweet, pure air and water of the Sierras, and setting these poor captives down in the valley of death.

When they try to escape! Did it never occur to the United States to make a Reservation pleasant and healthy enough for an Indian to be content in? My word for it, if you will give him a place fit to live in, he will be willing to make his home there.

I know nothing in history so dark and dreadful as the story of the Indians in this dreaded and deadly Reservation of the valley. The Indians surrendered on condition that they should be taken to good homes and taught the ways of the white man. Once in the white man's power, the chains began to tighten, tighten at every step. Once there, they were divided into lots, families torn apart, and put to work under guard; men stood over them with loaded muskets. The land was full of malaria. These men of the mountains began to sicken, to die; to die by degrees,—to die, as the hot weather came on, by hundreds. At last a few of the strongest, the few still able to stand, broke away and found their way back to the mountains. They were like living skeletons, skin and bone only, hollow-eyed and horrible to look upon. Toward the last, these poor Indians had crawled on their hands and knees to get back. They were followed by the soldiers, and taken wherever they could be found; taken back to certain death. One, a young man, still possessed of a little strength, fought with sticks and stones with all his might as he lay in the trail where he had fallen in his flight. He lifted his two bony hands between the foe and his dying old father. The two were taken and chained together. That night the young man with an old pair of scissors, which he had borrowed on pretense of wanting to trim his hair, killed the old man by pushing one of the points into his heart. You could see by the marks of blood on the young man's hand next morning, that he had felt more than once to see if the old man was quite dead. Then he drove the point of the scissors in his own heart, and crawled upon the old man's body, embraced it and died there. And yet all this had been done so quietly that the two guards who marched back and forth only a few feet distant, did not know till next morning that anything of the kind had been. Sometimes these wretches would beg, and even steal, on their way back from the dreadful Reservation. They were frightful, terrible, at such times. They sometimes stood far off outside the gate, and begged with outstretched hands. Their appearances were so against them, hungry, dying; and then this traditional hatred of four hundred years.

But this is too much digression. John Logan knew all the wrongs of his people only too well. He sympathized with them. And this meant his own ruin. A few Indians had made their way back of late, and John Logan had harbored them while the authorities were in pursuit. This was enough. An order had been sent to bring in John Logan.

He knew of this, and that was why he

now stood all alert and on fire, as these two men came stealing through the bush and straight for him. Should he fire? To shoot, to shoot at, to even point a gun at a white man, is death to the Indian. A slave of the South had been ten-fold more safe in striking his master in the old days of slavery, than is an Indian on the border in defending his person against a white man.

The two children, like frightened pheasants, when the old one gives signs of danger, darted down behind him, quick as thought, still as death. Their desperate and destitute existence in that savage land had made them savages in their cunning and caution. They said no word, made no sign. Their eyes were fixed on his every step and motion. He signaled them back. They darted like squirrels behind trees, and up and on through the thicket, toward the steep and inaccessible bluffs above. The two men saw the retreating children. They wanted Carrie. They darted forward; one of them jerked out and held up a paper in the face of John Logan.

"We want you at the Reservation. Come!"

Phin Emens stood full before Logan. He

shook the paper in his face. The man did not move. Carrie was fast climbing up the mountain. She was about to escape. Gar Dosson was furious. He attempted to pass, to climb the mountain, and to get at the girl. Still Logan kept himself between as he slowly retreated.

"Stand aside, and let me get that girl. I must take *her*, too!" shouted Dosson. Still Logan kept the man back. And now the children had escaped. Wild with rage, Dosson caught Logan by the shoulder and shouted, "Come!" With a blow that might have felled an ox, the Indian brought the man to the ground. Then, grasping his rifle in his right hand, he darted through the thicket after the retreating children, up the mountain, while Phin Emens stooped over his fallen friend.

CHAPTER III.

MAN-HUNTERS.

"*He caused the dry land to appear.*
—BIBLE.

The mountains from that fearful first
Named day were God's own house. Behold,
'Twas here dread Sinai's thunders burst
And showed His face. 'Twas here of old
His prophets dwelt. Lo, it was here
The Christ did come when death drew near.

Give me God's wondrous upper world
That makes familiar with the moon
These stony altars they have hurled
Oppression back, have kept the boon
Of liberty. Behold, how free
The mountains stand, and eternally.

SUCCESS makes us selfish. The history of the world chronicles no prosperity like that of ours; and so, thinking of only ourselves and our success, we forget others. It is easy, indeed, to forget the misery of others; and we hate to be told of it, too.

On a high mountain side overlooking the valley, hung a little camp like a bird's nest. It was hidden there in the densest wood, yet it looked out over the whole land. No bird, indeed no mother of her young, ever chose a deeper or wilder retreat, or a place more utterly apart from the paths and approaches of mankind.

Certainly the little party had stood in imminent peril of capture, and had prized freedom dearly indeed, to climb these crags and confront the very snow-peaks in their effort to make certain their safety.

And a little party, too, it must have been; for you could have passed within ten feet of the camp and not discovered it by day. And by night? Well, certainly by night no man would peril his life by an uncertain footing on the high cliffs here, only partly concealed by the thick growth of chaparral, topt by tall fir and pine and cedar and tamarack. And so a little fire was allowed to burn at night, for it was near the snow and always cold. And it was this fire, perhaps, that first betrayed the presence of the fugitives to the man-hunters.

Very poor and wretched were they, too. If

they had had more blankets they might not have so needed the fire. So poor were they, in fact, that you might have stood in the very heart of the little camp and not discovered any property at all without looking twice. A little heap of ashes in the center sending up a half-smothered smoke, two or three loose California lion-skins, thrown here and there over the rocks, a pair of moccasins or two, a tomahawk—and that was almost all. No cooking utensils had they—for what had they to cook? No eating utensils—for what had they to eat?

Great gnarled and knotty trees clung to the mountain side beyond, and a little to the left a long, thin cataract, which, from the valley far below, looked like a snowy plume, came pitching down through the tree tops. It had just been let loose from the hand of God—this sheen of shining water. Back and beyond all this, a peak of snow, a great pyramid and shining shaft of snow, with a crown of clouds, pierced heaven.

Stealthily, and on tip-toe, two armed men, both deeply disguised in great black beards, and in good clothes, stepped into this empty little camp. Bending low, looking right, looking left, guns in hand and hand on trigger, they stopped in the centre of the little camp, and looked cautiously up, down, and all around. Seeing no one, hearing nothing, they looked in each others' eyes, straightened up, and, standing their guns against a tree, breathed more freely in the gray twilight. Wicked, beastly-looking men were they, as they stood there loosening their collars, taking in their breath as if they had just had a hard climb, and looking about cautiously; hard, cruel and cunning, they seemed as if they partook something of the ferocity of the wild beasts that prowled there at night.

These two large animal-looking men were armed with pistols also. But at the belt of each hung and clanked and rattled something more terrible than any implement of death.

These were manacles! Irons! Chains for human hands!

Did it never occur to you as a little remarkable, that man only forges chains and manacles for his fellow-man? A cage will do for a wild beast, cattle are put in pens, bears in a pit, but man must be chained. Men carry these manacles with them only when they set out to take their fellow-man. These two men were man-hunters.

Standing there, manacles in hand, half beast and half devil, they were in the employment of the United States. They were sent to take John Logan, Carrie and Johnny, to the Reservation—the place most hated, dreaded, abhorred of all earthly places, the Reservation! Back of these two men lay a deeper, a more damning motive for the capture of the girl than the United States was really responsible for; for the girl, as we have seen, was very beautiful. This rare wild flower had now almost matured in the hot summer sun just past. But remember, it was all being done in the name of and under the direction of, and, in fact, by, the United States Government.

To say nothing of the desire of agents and their deputies to capture and possess beautiful girls, it is very important to any Indian agent that each victim, even though he be half or three-quarters, or even entirely, white, be kept on the Reservation; for every captive is so much money in the hands of the Indian agent. He must have Indians, as said before, to report to the Government in order to draw blankets, provisions, clothes, and farming utensils for them. True, the Indians do not get a tithe of these things, but he must be on the Reservation roll-call in order that the agent may draw them in his name.

This agency had become remarkably thin of Indians. The mountain Indians, accustomed to pure water and fresh air, could not live long in the hot, fever-stricken valley. They died by hundreds. And then, as if utterly regardless of the profits of the agents of the Reservation, they hung themselves in their prison-pens, with their own chains. Two, father and son, killed themselves with the same knife one night while chained together.

There was just a little bit of the old Roman in these liberty-loving natures, it seemed to me. See the father giving himself the death-wound, and then handing the knife to his son! The two chained apart, but still able to grasp each other's hands; grasping hands and dying so! Very antique that, it seems to me, in its savage valor—love of liberty, and lofty contempt of death. But then it was only Indians, and happened so recently.

It is true, Gar Dosson wanted revenge and the girl; and the two men wanted the little farm. Yet do not forget that back of all this lay that granite and immovable mountain of fact, that other propelling principle to compel them on to the hunt, the order, the sanction—the gold—of the government. Let it be told with bowed head, with eyes to the ground, and cheeks crimson with shame! Think of one of these hunted human beings—a beautiful young girl, just at that sweet and tender, almost holy period of life, the verge of womanhood, when every man of the land should start up with a noble impulse to throw the arm of protection about her!

"Shoo! they must be close about," began the shorter of the two ruffians, reaching back for his gun, as if he had heard something.

"No. Did n't you see that squirrel shucking a hazel nut on that rock there, just afore we came in?" said the other.

"A bushy-tailed gray? Yes, seed him scamper up a saplin."

"Wal, don't you know that if they had a bin hereabouts, a squirrel wouldn't a sot down there to shuck a nut?"

"Right! You've been among Injins so long that you know more about them than they do themselves."

"Wal, what I don't know about an Injin no one don't know. They've gone for grub, and will come back at sun-down."

"Come back here at sun-down?"

"Don't you see the skins there? Whar kin they sleep? They'll come afore dark, for even an Injin can't climb these rocks after dark. And when the gal's in camp, and that feller fixed—eh? eh?" And he tapped and rattled the manacles.

"Eh? eh? old Toppy?" and the two men poked each other in the ribs, and looked the very villians that they were.

"But let's see what they've got here. Two tiger-skins, an old moccasin and a tomahawk;" he looked at the handle and read the name, JOHN LOGAN; "Guess I'll hide that," said the agent, as he kicked the skins about, and then stuck the tomahawk up under his belt. "Guess that's about all."

"Guess that's about all!" sneered the other; "that's about all you know about Injuns. Allers got your nose to the ground, too. Look here!" And the man, who had been walking about and looking up in the trees, here drew down a bundle from the boughs of a fir.

"Well, I 'll swar! ef you can 't find things where a coon dog could n't!"

"Find things!" exclaimed the other, as he prepared to examine the contents of the bundle; "all you 've got to do is to look into a fir-tree in an Injun's camp. You see, bugs and things won't climb a fir gum; nothing but a red-bellied squirrel will go up a fir gum, for fear of sticking in the wax; and even a squirrel won't, if there is a string tied around, for fear of a trap. Wal, there is the string. So you see an Injun's *cache* is as safe up a fir-tree as under lock and key. Ah, they 're awful short of grub. Look thar! Been gnawing that bone, and they 've put that away for their suppers, I swar!"

"Wal, the grub is short, eh? They 'll be rather thin, I 'm thinking."

The other did not notice this remark, but throwing the bundle aside, he rose up and went back to the tree.

"By the beardy Moses! Look thar!" and

the man looked about as if half frightened, and then held up a bottle.

"Whisky?" asked the other, springing eagerly forward.

"No," answered the man, contemptuously, after smelling the bottle.

"Water, eh?" queried the other, with disgust.

"Wine! And look here. Do you know what that means? It means a white man! Yes, it does. No Injin ever left a cork in a bottle. Now, you look sharp. There will be a white man to tackle."

"Wal, I guess he won't be much of a white man, or he'd have whisky."

"Shoo! I heard a bird fly down the canyon. Somebody's a comin' up thar."

"We better git, eh?" said the other, getting his gun; "lay for 'em."

"Lay low and watch our chance. Maybe we'll come in on 'em friendly like, if there's white men. We're cattle men, you know; men hunting cattle," says the other, getting his gun and leading off behind the crags in the rear. "Leave me to do the talking. I'll tell a thing, and you'll swear to it. Wait, let's see," and he approaches the edge of the rocks, and, leaning over, looked below.

"See 'em?"

"Shoo! Look down there. The gal! She's a fawn. She's as pretty as a tiger-lily. Ah, my beauty!"

The other man stood up, shook his head thoughtfully, and seemed to hesitate. The watcher still kept peering down; then he turned and said: "The white man is old Forty-nine. He comes a bobbin' and a limpin' along with a keg on his back, and a climbin' up the mountain sidewise, like a crab."

"Whoop! I have it. It's wine, and they'll get drunk. Forty-nine will get drunk, don't you see, and then?"

"You're a wise 'un! Shake!" And they grasped hands.

"You bet! Now this is the little game. The gal and Logan, and the boy, will get here long first. Well, now, maybe we will go for the gal and the boy. But if we don't, we just lay low till all get sot down, and at that keg the old man's got, and then we just come in. Cattle-men, back in the mountains, eh?"

"That's the game. But here they come!

Shoo!" and with his finger to his lip the leader stole behind the rocks, both looking back over their shoulders, as Carrie entered the camp.

Her pretty face was flushed from exertion, and brown as a berry where not protected by the shock of black hair. She swung a broad straw hat in her hand, and tossed her head as if she had never worn and never would wear any other covering for it than that so bountifully supplied by nature. She danced gaily, and swung her hat as she flew about the little camp, and called at her chubby cherub of a brother over her shoulder. At last, puffing and blowing, and wiping his forehead, he entered camp and threw himself on one of the rocks.

"Why, you ain't tired, are you Johnny?"

"Oh, oh, oh,—no, I—I—I ain't tired a bit!" and he wiped his brow, and puffed and blowed, in spite of all his efforts to restrain himself.

"Why you like to climb the mountains, Johnny. Don't you know you said you liked to climb the mountains better than to eat?"

"Oh, yes, yes—I—I like to climb a mountain. That is, I like to climb one mountain at a time. But when there are two or three mountains all piled up on top of one another, Oh, oh, oh!"

"Oh, Johnny! You to go to bragging about climbing mountains! You can 't climb mountains!" And again the girl, with shoes that would hardly hold together, a dress in ribbons, and a face not unfamiliar with the dirt of the earth, danced back and forth before him and sung snatches of a mountain song. "Oh, I 'm so happy up here, Johnny. I always sing like a bird up here." Then, looking in his face, she saw that he was very thoughtful; and stepping back, and then forward, she said: "Why, what makes you so serious? They won't never come up here, will they, Johnny? Not even if somebody at the Reservation wanted me awful bad, and somebody gave somebody lots of money to take me back, they could n't never come up here, could they, Johnny?" And the girl looked eagerly about.

"Oh, no, Carrie, you are safe here. Why, you are as safe here as in a fort."

"This mountain is God's fort, John Logan says, Johnny. It is for the eagles to live in and the free people to fly to; for my people to climb up out of danger and talk to the Great Spirit that inhabits it." The girl clasped her hands and looked up reverently as she said this. "But come, now, Johnny, don't be serious, and I will sing you the nicest song I know till Forty-nine comes up the mountain; and I will dance for you, Johnny, and I will do all that a little girl can do to make you glad and happy as I am, Johnny."

Here John Logan came up the hill, and the girl stopped and said, very seriously,

"And you are right sure, John Logan, nobody will get after us again?—nobody follow us away up here, jam up, nearly against Heaven?"

Here the two men looked out.

"No, Carrie, nobody will ever climb this high for you,—nobody, except *somebody* that loves you very much, and loves you very truly."

"Injins might, but white men won't, I guess; too stiff in the jints!"

And again the girl whirled and danced

about, as if she had not heard one word he said. Yet she had heard every word, and heeded, too, for her eyes sparkled, and she danced even lighter than before; for her heart was light, and the wretched little outcast was—for a rare thing in her miserable life—very, very happy.

"I ain't stiff in the jints, am I, Johnny?" and she tapped her ankles.

"Carrie, sing me that other song of yours, and that will make my heart lighter," said Johnny.

"Why, Johnny, we haven't even got the clouds to overshadow us here; we're above the clouds, and everything else. But I'll sing for you if I can only make you glad as you was before they got after us." And throwing back her hair and twisting herself about, looking back over her shoulder and laughing, looking down at her ragged feet, and making faces, she began.

Like the song of a bird, her voice rang out on the coming night; for it was now full twilight, and the leaves quivered overhead; and far up and down the mountains the melody floated in a strange, sweet strain, and with a touch of tenderness that moved her companions to tears. Logan stood aside, looking down for Forty-nine a moment, then went to bring wood for the fire.

As her song ended, Carrie turned to the boy; but in doing so her eyes rested on the empty bottle left by the side of a stone spread with a tiger skin, by the two men. The boy had his head down, as if still listening, and did not observe her. She stopped suddenly, started back, looked to see if observed by her brother, and seeing that he was still absorbed she advanced, took up the bottle and held it up, glancing back and up the tree.

"Somebody's been here! Somebody's been here, and it's been white men; the bottle's empty."

She hastily hid the bottle, and stepping back and looking up where her little store had been hidden, she only put her finger to her lip, shook her head on seeing what had happened, and then went and stood by her little brother. Very thoughtful and full of care was she now. All her merriment had gone. She stood there as one suddenly grown old.

"Oh, thank you, Carrie. It's a pretty

song. But what can keep Forty-nine so long?"

The boy rose as he said this, and turning aside looked down the mountain into the gathering darkness. The girl stood close beside him, as if afraid.

"He is coming. Far down, I hear Forty-nine's boots on the bowlders."

"Oh, I'm so glad! And I'm so glad he's got pistols!" said the girl, eagerly. The two men, who had stepped out, looked at each other as she said this and made signs.

"Why, Carrie, are you afraid here! You are all of a tremble!" said the boy, as she clung close to him, when they turned back.

"Johnny," said the girl eagerly, almost wildly, as she looked around, "if men were to come to take us to that Reservation, what would you do?"

"What would I do? I would kill 'em! Kill 'em dead, Carrie. I would hold you to my heart so, with this arm, and with this I would draw my pistol so, and kill 'em dead."

The two heads of the man-hunters disappeared behind the rocks. The boy pushed back the girl's black, tumbled stream of hair from her brow, and kissing her very tenderly, he went aside and sat down; for he was very, very weary.

A twilight squirrel stole out from the thicket into the clearing and then darted back as if it saw something only partly concealed beyond. The two children saw this, and looked at each other half alarmed. Then the girl, as if to calm the boy—who had grown almost a man in the past few weeks—began to talk and chatter as if she had seen nothing, suspected nothing.

"When the Winter comes, Johnny, we can't stay here; we would starve."

"Carrie, do the birds starve? Do the squirrels starve? What did God make us for if we are to starve?"

All this time the two men had been stealing out from their hiding-place, as if resolved to pounce upon and seize the girl before Forty-nine arrived. The leader had signaled and made signs to his companion back there in the gloaming, for they dared not speak lest they should be heard; and now they advanced stealthily, guns in hand, and now they fell back to wait a better chance; and just as they were about to spring upon the two from behind, the snowy white head of old Forty-nine blossomed above the rocks, and his red face, like a great opening flower, beamed in upon the little party, while the good-natured old man puffed and blowed as he fanned himself with his hat and sat down his keg of provisions. And still he puffed and blowed, as if he would never again be able to get his breath. The two men stole back.

"And Forty-nine likes to climb the mountains too, don't he? Good for his health. See, what a color he's got! And see how fat he is! Good for your health, ain't it, papa Forty-nine?"

But the good old miner was too hot and puffy to answer, as the merry little girl danced with delight around him.

"Why, it makes you blow, don't it? Strange how a little hill like that could make a man blow," said Johnny, winking at Carrie.

But old Forty-nine only drew a long, thin wild flower through his hand, and looked up now and then to the girl. He beckoned her

to approach, and she came dancing across to where he sat.

"It's a sad looking flower, and it's a small one. But, my girl, the smallest flower is a miracle. And, Carrie, sometimes the sweetest flowers grows closest to the ground."

The man handed her the flower, and was again silent. His face had for a moment been almost beautiful. Here Logan came up with a little wood.

"Oh, John Logan, what a pretty flower for your button-hole!" and the fond girl bounded across and eagerly placed it in the young man's breast.

The old man on the keg saw this, and his face grew dark. His hands twisted nervously, and he could hardly keep his seat on his keg. Then he hitched up his pants right and left, sat down more resolutely on the keg than before, but said nothing for a long time.

At last the old man hitched about on his keg, and said sharply, over his shoulder: "I saw a track, a boot-track, coming up. On the watch, there!"

The others looked about as if alarmed. It was now dark. Suddenly the two men ap-

peared, looking right and left, and smiling villainously. They came as if they had followed Forty-nine, and not from behind the rocks, where they had been secreted.

"Good evenin', sir! good evenin', sir! Going to rain, eh? Heard it thunder, and thought best to get shelter. Cattle-men—we're cattle-men, pard and I. Seed your camp-fire, and as it was thunderin,' we came right in. All right, boss? All right, eh? All right?" And the man, cap in hand, bowed from one to the other, as not knowing who was the leader, or whom he should address.

"All right," answered Logan. "You're very welcome. Stand your guns there. You're as welcome under these trees as the birds—eh, Forty-nine?"

But Forty-nine was now silent and thoughtful. He was still breathless, and he only puffed and blowed his answer, and sat down on his keg again with all his might.

"You must be hungry," said the girl kindly, approaching the men.

"Heaps of provisions," puffed Forty-nine, and again he half arose and then sat down on his keg, tighter and harder, if possible, than before.

"Thank you, gents, thank you. It's hungry we are—eh, pard?"

"We'll have a spread right off," answered the good hearted Logan, now spreading a rock, which served for a table, with the food; when he observed the two men look at the girl and make signs. He looked straight and hard at the man-hunters for a moment, and seeing them exchange glances and nod their ill-looking heads at each other he suddenly dropped his handful of things and started forward. He caught the leader by the shoulder, and whirling him about as he stood there with his companion leering at the girl, he cried out:

"Hunting cattle, are you? What's your brand? What's the brand of your cattle, I say? I know every brand in Shasta. Now what is your brand?"

Johnny had strode up angrily toward the two men, and followed them up as they retreated. Old Forty-nine, who now was on the alert, and had his sleeves rolled up almost to his elbows from the first, had not been indifferent, but was reaching his tremendous fist towards the retreating nose of Dosson. Yet it was too dark to distinguish friend from foe.

"Why, we are not rich men, stranger. We are poor men, and have but few cattle, and so, so we have no brand—eh? pardner—eh?"

"No. We got no brand. Poor men, poor men."

"We are poor men, with a few cattle that have gone astray. We are hungry, tired poor men, that have lost their way in the night. Poor men that 's hungry, and now you want to drive us out into the storm."

"Oh, Forty-nine,—John Logan,—they're poor hungry men!" interposed Carrie.

"There, there 's my hand!" cried impulsive, honest old Forty-nine. "That 's enough. You 're hungry. Sit down there. And quick, Carrie, pour us the California wine. Here 's a gourd, there 's a yeast powder can, and there's a tin cup. Thank you. Here's to you. Ah, that sets a fellow all right. It warms the heart; and, I beg your pardon—it's mean to be suspicious. Here, fill us up again. Ah, that 's gone just to the spot! Eh, fellows?"

"To the right spot! Keep him a drinkin',

and the others, too," whispered Dosson to Emens.

"That 's the game!" And the two villains winked at each other, and slapped Forty-nine on the back, and laughed, and pretended to be the best friend he had in the world.

The two men now sat at the table, and Carrie and Johnny bustled about and helped them as they ate and drank. Meantime Logan went for more wood to make a light.

"And here 's the bread, and here 's the meat, and—and—that 's about all there is," said the girl at last. Then she stood by and with alarm saw the men swallow the last mouthful, and feel about over the table and look up to her for more in the dark.

"All there is? All gone?"

"Yes, and to-morrow, Johnny?"

"To-morrow, Carrie?" called out Forty-nine, who was now almost drunk: "We 've had a good supper, let to-morrow take care of itself. Eh! Let to-morrow take care of itself! That's my motto—hic—divide the troubles of the year up into three hundred and sixty-five parts, and take the pieces one at a time. Live one day at a time. That's my philosophy." And the poor old man, Forty-nine, held his hat high in the air, and began to hiccough and hold his neck unsteadily.

The girl saw this with alarm. As if by accident she placed herself between the men and their guns. Meantime, the two men were trying in vain to get at the pistols of Forty-nine. They would almost succeed, and then, just as they were about to get hold of them, the drunken man would roll over to the other side or change position. All the time Carrie kept wishing so devoutly that Logan would come.

"Take a drink," said one of the men to the girl, reaching out his cup, after glancing at his companion. But the girl only shook her head, and stepped further back. "Thought you said she was civilized?" "She, she is civilized; but isn 't quite civilized enough to get drunk yet," hiccoughed Forty-nine, as he battered his tin-cup on the table, and again foiled the hand just reached for his pistol. The boy saw this, and stole back through the dark behind his sister. To remove the cap and touch his tongue to the tubes of the guns was the work only of a second, and again he was back by the side of the men. Eagerly all the time the girl kept looking over her shoulders into the dark, deep woods, for Logan. The thunder rolled, and it began to grow very dark. She went up to Forty-nine, on pretense of helping him to more wine, and whispered sharply in his ear.

The old man only stared at her in helpless wonder. His head rolled from one side to the other like that of an idiot. His wits were utterly under water.

And now, as the darkness thickened and the men's actions could hardly be observed, one of them pushed the drunken man over, clutched his pistols, and the two sprang up together.

"I 've got 'em, Gar," cried Emens, and the two started back for their guns. The girl stood in the way, and Dosson threw his massive body upon her and bore her to the earth, while the other, awkwardly holding the two pistols in one hand, groped in the dark for their guns.

The storm began to beat terribly. The mountains fairly trembled from the rolling thunder. As the man was about to clutch the guns, he felt rather than saw that a tall figure stood between. That instant a flash of lightning showed John Logan standing there, the boy by his side, and two ugly pistols thrust forward. The man-hunters were unmasked in the fiery light of heaven, and Logan knew them for the first time.

"I will not kill you." He said this with look and action that was grand and terrible. "Take your guns and go! Out into the storm! If God can spare you, I can spare you. Go!"

And by the lightning's light, the two men, with two ugly pistol-nozzles in their faces, took their guns and groped and backed down the mountain into the darkness, where they belonged.

CHAPTER IV.

THE OLD GOLD-HUNTER.

"For the Right! as God has given
Man to see the Maiden Right!"
For the Right, through thickest night,
Till the man-brute Wrong be driven
From high places; till the Right
Shall lift like some grand beacon light.

For the Right! Love, Right and duty;
Lift the world up, though you fall
Heaped with dead before the wall;
God can find a soul of beauty
Where it falls, as gems of worth
Are found by miners dark in earth.

Old Forty-nine had not cast his life and lot with John Logan at all. Yet this singular and contradictory old man stood ready to lay down his seemingly worthless life at a moment's notice for this boy whom he had almost brought up from childhood. But he was not living with him in the mountains. He had done all he could to protect him, to shelter and feed him, all the time. But now the pursuit was so hot and desperate that the old man, in his sober moments—rare enough, I admit—began to doubt if it would be possible to save this young man much longer from the clutches of the Agents. Indeed, it was only by the sweet persuasion of Carrie that he had this time been induced to go with her and Johnny up on the spur of the mountain, and there meet John Logan with some provisions. From there he was persuaded to go with him to his hiding-place, high up the mountain, where we left him in the last chapter.

But the poor old man's head was soon under water again, as we have seen. That keg of California wine and the few bits of bread and meat, which so suddenly disappeared in the hands of Dosson and Emens, were all he happened to have in the cabin when the two children came in at dusk. But these he had snatched up at once and ran with them to Logan.

But the next morning, when his head was once more above water, and he had been told all that had happened, he pulled his long white beard to the right and to left, and at last rose up and took the two children and led them back down the steep and stupendous mountain to his cabin. He knew that John Logan was now a doomed man. Had he been alone, had there been no one but himself and this hunted man, he would have stayed by his side. As it was, it made the old man a year older to decide. And it was like tearing his heart out by the roots, when he rose up, choking with agony, grasped Logan's hand, bade him farewell, and led the children hurriedly away. Once, twice, the old man stopped and turned suddenly about, and looked sharply and almost savagely up the mountains, as if to return. And then, each time he sighed, shook his head, and hurried on down the hill. He held tightly on to the little brown hands of the children, as if he feared that they, too, like himself, might let their better natures master them, and so turn back and join the desolate and hunted man.

That evening, after the old man had returned from his tunnel, and while he prepared a meager meal from a few potatoes and a heel of bacon found back in the corner of a shelf, and so hard that even the wood-rats had refused to eat it, a passing fellow-miner put his heavy head and shoulders in at the half open cabin and shouted out that a barn had been burned in the valley, a house fired into, and the tomahawk of John Logan found hard by. The children glanced at each other by the low fire-light. But old Forty-nine only went on with his work as the head withdrew and passed on, but he said never a word. He was very thoughtful all the evening. He was now perfectly certain that his course had been the wise one, the only prudent one in fact. Logan he knew was now beyond help. He must use all his art and address to keep the children from further peril. He made them promise to remain in his cabin, to never attempt to reach Logan. He told them that their presence with him would only greatly embarrass him in his flight; that they might be followed if they attempted to reach him, and that he and they would then be taken and sent to the Reservation together. But he told them further —and their black eyes flashed like fire as he spoke in a voice tremulous with emotion and earnestness—that if ever Logan came to that cabin hungry, or for help of any kind, they should help him with every means in their power.

And so the old man went back to work in his tunnel; and as the autumn wore away and winter drew on, the children kept close about the little old cabin, waiting, waiting, waiting; looking up toward the now white, cold mountain, yet obeying Forty-nine to the letter.

Meantime the man-hunt went on; although the children knew nothing for a long time of the deadly energy with which it was conducted.

What a strange place for two bright, budding children was this old, old cabin, with its old, old man, and its dark and miserable interior! How people shunned the lonely old place, and how it sank down into the earth and among the weeds and willows, and long strong yellow tangled grass, as if it wanted to be shunned!

On a dirty old shelf near the fire-place lay a torn and tattered book. It was thumbed and thrumbed all to pieces from long and patient use. When the wind blew through the chinks of the cabin, this old book seemed to have life. It fluttered there like a wounded bird. Its leaves literally whispered. This old book was a Bible.

More houses had been burned in the little valley, and the crime laid to John Logan. He had now been proclaimed an outlaw in effect by every settler. Those two men had made him so odious that many settlers had vowed to shoot him on sight. Dosson at last went before a magistrate and swore that John Logan had shot at him while in the performance of his duty as a sub-agent of the Reservation. By this means he procured a warrant for his arrest by the civil authorities, to be placed in the hands of the newly elected sheriff of the newly organized and sparsely settled country. Things looked desperate indeed. To add to the agony of the crisis, a sharp and bitter winter now wrapped the whole world in snow and ice. It was no longer possible for any one to subsist in the mountains, or survive at all without fire and fire-arms. These the hunted man did not dare use. They were witnesses that would betray his presence, and must not be thought of.

All this time the old man and the children

could do nothing. The children hovered over the fire in the wretched old cabin. And what a cold, cheerless place it was!

But if the interior of this old cabin was gloomy, that of the old tunnel was simply terrible. Yet in this dark and dreadful place the old man had spent nearly a quarter of a century.

I wonder if the glad, gay world knows where it gets its gold? Does that fair woman, or well-clad, well-fed man, know anything about the life of the gold-hunter? When the gold is brought to the light and given to the commerce of the world, we see it shining in the sun. It is now a part of the wealth of the nation. But do not forget that every piece of gold you touch or see, or stand credited with at your bank, cost some brave man blood, life!

This old Forty-nine, years before, when the camp was young, had found a piece of gold-bearing quartz in a ledge on the top of a high, sharp ridge, that pointed down into the canyon. This was before quartz mining had been thought of. But the shrewd, thoughtful man saw that from this source came all the gold in the placer. He could see that it was from this vein that all the fine gold in the camp had been fed. He resolved to strike at the fountain head. It was by accident he had made his discovery. The high, sharp and narrow ridge was densely timbered, and now that the miners had settled in the canyon below, the annual fires would not be allowed to sweep over the country, and the woods would soon be almost impenetrable. So argued Forty-nine. For all his mind was bent on keeping his secret till he could pierce the mountains from the canyon-level below, and strike the ledge in the heart of the great high-backed ridge, where he felt certain the gold must lay in great heaps and flakes and wedges. And so it was with a full heart and a strong arm that he had begun his low, dark tunnel—all alone at the bottom of the ridge.

He had begun his tunnel in a secluded place, under a tuft of dense wood, on the steep hillside. He made the mouth of the tunnel very low and narrow. At first he wheeled out the dirt in his wheelbarrow only when the water in the canyon was high enough to carry off the earth which he excavated. He worked very hard and kept very sober for a long time.

Day after day he expected to strike the ledge.

But day after day, week after week, month after month, stole away between his fingers, and still no sign of the ledge. A year went by. Then he struck a hard wall of granite. This required drills, fuse-powder, and all the appliance of the quarry. He had to stop work now and then and wash in the fast failing placers, to get money enough to continue his tunnel. Besides, he now could make only a few inches headway each week. Sometimes he would be a whole month making the length of his pick-handle.

All this was discouraging. The man began to grow heart-sick. Who was there at home waiting and waiting all this time? No one in the camp could say. In fact, no one in the camp knew any thing at all about this silent man, who seemed so superior to them all; and as the camp knew nothing at all of the man, either his past or his present, as is usually the case, it made a history of its own for him. And you may be certain it was not at all complimentary to this exclusive and silent man of the tunnel.

Two, three, four, five years passed. The

camp had declined; miners had either gone back to the States, gone to new mines, or gone up on the little hill out of the canyon to rest together; and yet this man held on to his tunnel. He was a little bit bent now from long stooping, waiting, toiling, and there were ugly crows-feet about his eyes—eyes that had grown dim and blood-shot from the five years glare of the single candle in that tunnel.

And the man was not so exclusive now. The tunnel was now no secret. It was spoken of now with derision, only to be laughed at.

Six, seven, eight, nine, ten years! The man has grown old. He is bent and gray. But his faith, which the few remaining miners call a madness, is still unbroken. Yet it is not in human nature to endure all this agony of suspense, all this hope deferred from day to day, week to week, month to month, year to year, and still be human. The man has, in some sense, become a brute. He now is seen to reel and totter to his cabin, late at night oftentimes. He has at last fallen into the habit of the camp. He can drink, gamble, carouse, as late as the latest.

Now and then, it is true, he has his sober

spells, and all the good of his great nature is to the surface. Now he takes up a map and diagram which is hidden under the broad stone of the hearth, and examines it, measures and makes calculations by the hour at night, when all the camp is, or ought to be, asleep.

Maybe it is the placing and displacing of this great stone that has given rise to the story in the camp that the old man is not so poor as he pretends. Maybe some of the rough men who hang about the camp have watched him through the chink-holes in the wretched cabin some night, and decided that it is gold which he keeps concealed under the great hearth-stone.

Eleven, twelve, thirteen, fourteen, fifteen years! The man's hair is long and hangs in strings. It is growing gray, almost white. Some men have been trying to get into the bent old man's cabin at night to find the buried treasure. The old man's double-barreled shot-gun has barked in their faces; and there has been a thinly attended funeral. The camp is low, miserable. The tide is out. Wrecks of rockers, toms, sluices, flumes, derricks, battered pans, tom-irons, cradles, old cabin, strew the sandy strand.

This last act has left the old man utterly alone; yet he is seen even more frequently than before at the "Deadfall." Is he trying to forget that man had died at his hand?

Now and then you see him leading a tawny boy about, and talking in a low, tender way of better things than his life and appearance would indicate. The man is still on the down grade. And yet how long he has been on this decline! One would say he should be at the bottom by this time.

When we reflect how very far a man can fall, we can estimate something of the height in which he stands when fresh from his Maker's hand.

Sixteen, seventeen, eighteen, nineteen, twenty, twenty-one years! The iron-gray hair is white as the snow on the mountain-tops that environ him. The tall man is bent as a tree is bent when the winter snow lies heavily on its branches. The tawny boy is grown a man now. This is John Logan, the fugitive. The two homeless children have long since taken his place.

And still the pick clangs on in that dark, damp tunnel that is always dripping, dripping, dripping, where it looks out at the glaring day, as if in eternal tears for the wasted life within. Yet now there is hope.

New life has been infused into this old camp of late years. The tide is flowing in. The placer mines have perished and passed into history. But there is a new industry discovered. It is quartz mining—the very thing that this old man has given his life to establish. And it is this that has kept the old man up, alive, for the past few years. He is now certain that he will strike it yet.

Is there some one waiting still, far away? We do not know. He does not know now. Years and years ago, utterly discouraged, yet mechanically keeping on, he ceased to write.

But now these two new lives here have ran into his. If he could only strike it now! If he could only strike it for them!

It is mid-winter. The three are almost starving. Old Forty-nine has been prudent, cautious, careful of the two helpless waifs thrown into his hands. Could he, old, broken, destitute, friendless, stand up boldly between the man-hunters and these children? Impossible. And so it is that Dosson and Emens are not strangers at the old man's cabin now, hateful as is their presence there to all. They are allowed to come and go. And Dosson pays court to Carrie. They ply the old man with drink. The poor, broken, brave old miner, still dreams and hopes that he will strike it yet—and then! Sometimes he starts up in his sleep and strikes out with his bony hands—as if to expel them from his cabin and keep Carrie safe, sacred, pure. Then he sinks back with a groan, and Carrie bends over him and her great eyes fill with tears.

CHAPTER V.

THE CAPTURE.

O, the mockery of pity!
Weep with fragrant handkerchief,
In pompous luxury of grief,
Selfish, hollow-hearted city?

O these money-getting times!
What's a heart for? What's a hand,
But to seize and shake the land,
Till it tremble for its crimes?

MIDNIGHT, and the mighty trees knock their naked arms together, and creak and cry wildly in the wind. In Forty-nine's cabin, by a flickering log-fire, Carrie sits alone. The wind howls horribly, the door creaks, and the fire snaps wickedly; the wind roars—now the roar of a far-off sea, and now it smites the cabin in shocks, and sifts and shakes the snow through the shingle. The girl draws her tattered blanket tighter about her, and sits a little closer to the fire. Now there is a sudden, savage gust of wind, wilder, fiercer than before, and a sheet of snow sifts in through a crack in the door, and dances over the floor.

"What a storm!" exclaims the girl, as she rises up, looks about, and then takes the blanket from her shoulders and stuffs it in the crack by the door.

She listens, looks about again, and then, going up to the little glass tacked beside the fire-place, carefully arranges her splendid hair that droops down over her shoulders in the careless, perfect fashion of Evangeline.

"Heaven help any one who is out in this storm to-night!"

Then she takes another stick from the corner and places it on the fire.

"Forty-nine will be here soon, and Johnny; Johnny with news about him—about poor John Logan."

She shakes her head and clasps her hands.

"It is nearly half a year since that night. They can't take him—they dare not take him. They are hunting him—hunting him in this storm—hunting him as if he were a wild beast. He hides with the cattle in the sheds, with the very hogs in their pens. They come upon him there; he starts from his sleep and dashes away, while they follow, and track him by the blood of his feet in the snow. Oh, how terrible it is! I must not think of it; I will go mad."

She turns to the door and listens. She draws back the ragged curtains from the window and tries to look out into the storm. She can hear and see nothing, and she walks back again to the fire. "I must set them their supper." As she says this, she goes to a little cupboard and takes a piece of bread, puts it on a plate and sets it on the table. Then she places two plates and two cups of water. "They will be here soon, and they must have their suppers. Oh, that grocery!" She shudders as she says this. "And Johnny will bring me news of him—of John Logan. What's that?"

She springs to the door, lifts the latch, and Stumps steals in, brushing the snow from his neck and shoulders. He has a club in his hand, and looks back and about him as he shuts the door.

"Oh, sister, its awful! I tell you its too awful!"

"Brother—brother! What has happened?

What is awful? What is it, Johnny? And he, John Logan?"

"He's been there!" The boy shivers and points in a half-frightened manner toward the little hill. "Yes, he has; he's been up on the hill by his mother's grave; and he's been to 'Squire Field's house—yes, he has; and he couldn't get in, for they had a big dog tied to the gate, and now they have got another dog tied to the gate. Yes, and they tracked him all around by the blood in the snow!"

"Oh brother! don't, don't!"

"Don't be afraid, sister; he has gone away now. Oh, if he would only go away and stay away—far away, and they couldn't catch him, I'd be just as glad as I could be! Yes, I would; so help me, I would."

"And he has been up there, and in this storm!"

She speaks this to herself, as she goes to the window and attempts to look out.

"Poor, poor John Logan!" sighs the boy. "I wish his mother was alive; I do, so help me. She was a good woman, she was; she didn't sick Bose on me, she didn't."

As the boy says this he stands his club in the corner, and looks with his sister for a moment sadly into the fire, and then suddenly says:

"I'm hungry. Sister, ain't you got something to eat. Forty-nine, he's down to the grocery, and Phin Emens he's down to the grocery, too, and he swears awfully about John Logan, and he says it's the Injun that's in him that makes him so bad. Do you think it's the Injun that's in him, sister?"

As the boy says this, the girl turns silently to the little table and pushes it toward him.

"There, Johnny, that's all there is. You must leave some for Forty-nine."

"Poor, poor John Logan!"

He eats greedily for a moment, then stops suddenly and looks into the fire.

Carrie, also looking into the fire, murmurs:

"And Sylvia Fields let them tie a dog there to keep him away! I would have killed that dog first. If John Logan should come here, I would open that door—I would open that door to him!"—There is a dark and terrified face at the window—"And I would give him bread to eat, and let him sit by this fire and get warm !"

"And I would, too—so help me, I would!" The boy pushes back his bread, and rises and goes up to his sister. "Yes, I would. I don't care what Phin Emens, or anybody says; for his mother didn't sick 'Bose' at me, she didn't!"

The pale and pitiful face at the window begins to brighten. There is snow in the long matted black locks that fall to his shoulders. For nearly half a year this man has fled from his fellow-man, a hunted grizzly, a hunted tiger of the jungle.

What wonder that his step is stealthy as he lifts the latch and enters? What wonder that his eyes have an uncommon glare as he looks around, looks back over his shoulder as he shuts the door noiselessly behind him? What wonder that his clothes hang in shreds about him, and his feet and legs are bound in thongs; that his arms are almost bare; that his bloodless face is half hidden in black and shaggy beard?

"Carrie, I have come to you. Yours is the only door that will open to me now."

"John Logan!" She starts; the boy, too, utters a low, stifled cry. Then they draw near the miserable man. For they are bred of the woods, and have nerves of iron, and they know the need and the power of silence, too.

"*You* here, John Logan?" Carrie whispers, with a shudder.

"Ay, I am here—starving, dying!"

The boy takes up the bread he had dropped, and places it on the table before Logan. The hunted outcast sits down wearily and begins to eat with the greediness of a starved beast. The girl timidly brushes the snow from his hair, and takes a pin from her breast and begins to pin up a great rent in his shirt that shows his naked shoulder.

The boy is glad and full of heart, and of indescribable delight that he has given his bread to the starving man. He stands up, brightly, with his back to the fire for a moment, and then goes back and brushes off the snow from the man's matted hair, then back to the fire.

"I'm awful glad to see you eat, Mr. John Logan," says Stumps; "I wish there was more, I do," and he rocks on his foot and wags his head from shoulder to shoulder gleefully. "It ain't much—it ain't much, Mr. John Logan; but it is all there is."

"All there is, and they were eating it." The man says this aside to himself, and he hides his face for a moment, as if he would conceal a tear. Then, after a time he seems to recover himself, and he lays the bread down on the table, tenderly, silently, carefully indeed, as if it were the most delicate and precious thing on earth. Then, lifting his face, looks at them with an effort to be cheerful, and says:

"I—I forgot; I—I am not hungry. I have had my dinner. I—I, oh yes; I have been eating a great deal. Oh, no, no, no; I'm not hungry—not hungry!"

As the man says this he rises and stands between the others at the fire. He puts his hands over their heads, and looks alternately in their uplifted faces. There is a long silence. "Carrie, they have tied a dog to that door, over yonder."

"There is no dog tied to this door, John Logan."

Low and tender with love, yet very firm and earnest is her voice. And her eyes are lifted to his. He looks down into her soul, and there is an understanding between them. There is a conversation of the eyes too refined for words; too subtle, too sweet, too swift for words.

They stand together but a moment there, soul flowing into soul and tiding forth, and to and fro; but it was as if they had talked together for hours. He leans his head, kisses her lifted and unresisting lips, and says, "God bless you," and that is all.

It is her first kiss, the imprint, the mint-mark on this virgin gold. This maiden of a moment since, is a woman now.

"Do you know that they are after you?" The girl says this in a sort of wild whisper, as she looks toward the door.

"Do I know that they are after me? Father in Heaven, who should know it better than I?" The man throws up his arms, and totters back and falls into a seat from very weakness. "Do I know that they are after me? For more than half a year I have fled; night and day, and day and night I have fled, hidden away;

starting up at midnight from down among the cattle, where I had crept to keep warm; and then on, on and on, out into the snow, the storm, over the frozen ground, to the deep canyon and dark woods, where, naked and bleeding, I disputed with the bear for his bed in the hollow tree."

The boy springs to the door. Is it the storm that is tugging and rattling at the latch?

But the girl seems to see, to heed, to hear only John Logan. She clutches his hand in both her own and covers it with kisses and with tears.

"John Logan, I pity you! I—I—" she had almost said, "I love you."

"Thank Heaven! Thank Heaven for one true heart, and one true hand when all the world is against me! Carrie, I could die now content. The bitterness of my heart passes away, and the wild, mad nature that made me an Ishmaelite, with every man's hand against me, and my hand against all, is gone. I am another being. I could die now content;" and he bows his head.

"But you must not, you shall not die! You

must go—go far away; why hover about this place?"

"I do not know. But yonder lies the only being who ever befriended me; and somehow I get lonesome when I get far away from her grave. And I go round and round, like the sun around the world, and come back to where I started from."

"But you must go—go far away—go now."

"Do you know what you are saying? I was never outside of this. All would be strange. I would be lost, lost there. And then, do you not imagine they are waiting for me there—everywhere? Look at my face! This tinge of Indian blood, that all men abhor and fear, and call treacherous and bloody. Across my brow at my birth was drawn a brand that marks me forever—a brand—a brand as if it were the brand of Cain."

The man bows his head, and turns away.

Slowly and timidly Carrie approaches him, and she lays her hand on his arm and looks in his face. The boy still watches by the door.

"But you will fly from here?"

His arm drops over her hair, down to her

shoulder, and he draws her to his breast, as she looks up tenderly in his face, and pleads:

"You will go now—at once? For you will die here."

"Ah, I will die here." He says this with a calm and dogged determination. "Carrie, I have one wish, one request—only one. I know you are weak and helpless yourself, and can't do much, and I ought not to ask you to do anything."

Stumps has left the door as he hears the man mention that there is something to be done, and stands by their side.

"Whatever it is you ask, John Logan, we will do it—we will do it."

The girl says this with a firmness that convinces him that it will be done.

"We will do it! we will do it! so help me, we will do it!" blubbers Stumps.

"What is it, John Logan, we can do?"

"I will not fly from here." He looks down tenderly into their faces. Then he lifts his face. It is dark and terrible, and his lips are set with resolution. "I will die here. It may be to-night, it may be to-morrow. It may be as I turn to go out at that door they will send their bullets through my heart; it may be while I kneel in the snow at my mother's grave. But, sooner or later, it will come—it will come!"

"But please, John Logan, what is it we can do?"

Her voice is tremulous, and her eyes stream with tears.

"Carrie, I am a man—a strong man—and ought not to ask anything of a helpless girl. But I have no other friend. I have had no friends. All the days of my life have been dark and lonely. And now I am about to die, Carrie, I want you to see that I am buried by my mother yonder. I am so weary, and I could rest there. And then she, poor broken-hearted mother, she might not be so lonesome then. Do you promise?"

"I do promise!" and the boy echoes this scarcely audible but determined answer.

"Thank you—thank you! And now good night. I must be going, lest I draw suspicion on you. Good night, good night; God bless you, Carrie!"

He presses her to his heart, hastily embraces her, and tearing himself away, stoops and kisses the boy as he passes to the door. Drawing his tattered shirt closer about his shoulders, and turning his face as if to conceal his emotion, he lays his hand upon the latch to suddenly dart forth.

Two dark figures pass the window, and in a moment more the latch-string is clutched by a rough, unsteady hand from without.

"Here, here!" cries the girl, as she springs back to the dingy curtain that divides off a portion of the cabin into a bed-room. "Here! in here! Quick! quick!" as she draws the curtain aside, and lets it fall over the retreating fugitive. Forty-nine and Gar Dosson enter. The former is drunk, and therefore dignified and silent. His companion is drunk, and therefore garrulous and familiar. Wine floats a man's real nature nearly to the surface.

Forty-nine lifts his hat, bows politely and respectfully to the children, brushes his hat with his elbow as he meanders across the floor to the peg in the wall, but cannot quite trust himself to speak.

"Hullo, Carats!" cries Gar Dosson, as he chucks her under the chin. "Knowed I was coming, did n't you? Got yourself fixed up.

Pretty, ain't she?" and he winks a blood-shot eye toward Stumps. "And when is it going to be my Carats? Pretty soon, now, eh?" and he walks, or rather totters, aside.

"Umph! I have got 'em again, Carrie. Fly around and get us something to eat. Fly around, Carrie, fly around! Oh, I 've got the shakes again!" groans Forty-nine.

"Poor old boy!" and she brushes the snow from his beard and his tattered coat. "Why, Forty-nine, you 're shaking like a leaf."

"He's drunk—that's what's the matter with him." Gar Dosson growls this out between his teeth as he sets his gun in the corner.

"He's not drunk! Its the ager!" retorts Stumps fiercely.

Gar Dosson, glaring at the boy, steadies himself on his right leg, and diving deep in his left hand pocket, draws forth a large bill or poster. With both hands he manages to spread this out, and swaggering up to the wall near the window he hangs it on two pegs that are there to receive coats or hats.

"Look at that!" and he crookedly points with his crooked fingers at the large letters, and reads: "One thousand dollars (hic) dollars reward for the capture of John Logan! What do you say to that, Carats? That's a fine fellow to have for a lover, now, ain't it?—a waluable lover, now, ain't it? Worth a thousand dollars! Oh, don't I wish he was a-hanging around here now! Would n't I sell him, and get a thousand dollars, eh? Yes, I would. I just want that thousand dollars. And I'm the man that's going to get it, too! Eh, old Blossom-nose?" Forty-nine jerks back his dignified head as the bully gesticulates violently.

"You will, will you? Well, may-be you will (hic), but if you get a cent of that money (hic) for catching that man you don't enter that door again; no, you don't lift that latch-string again as long as old Forty-nine has a fist to lift!" and he thrusts his doubled hand hard into the boaster's face.

"Good for you!" cries Carrie. "Dear, good, brave old Forty-nine; I like you—I love you!" and the girl embraces him, while the boy flourishes his club at the back of the bully.

"No, don't you hit a man when he 's down, sah," continues Forty-nine. "That 's the true doctrine of a gentleman—the true doctrine of a gentleman, sah." He flourishes his hand, totters forward, totters back, and hesitates—"The true doctrine of a gentleman, sah. The little horse in the horse-race, sah—the bottom dog in the dog-fight, sah. The—"

And the poor old man totters back and falls helplessly in the great, home-made chair near the corner, where stands the gun. His head is under water.

"The true doctrines of a gentleman," snaps Dosson; and he throws out a big hand toward the drooping head. "Old Blossom-nose!" Then turning to Carrie. "The sheriff's a coming; he gave me that 'ere bill—yes, he did. He's down to the grocery, now. He's going around to all the cabins, and a-swearing 'em in a book, that they don't know nothing about John Logan. The sheriff, he's a comin' here, Carats, right off."

There is a rift in the curtain, and the pitiful face of the fugitive peers forth.

"The sheriff coming here!" He turns, feels the wall, and tries the logs with his hands. Not a door, not a window. Solid as the solid earth.

"Coming here? But what is he coming here for?" demands Carrie.

"Coming here to find out what you know about John Logan. Oh, he's close after him."

"Close after me!" gasps Logan. The man feels for something to lay hand upon by which to defend himself. "I will not be taken alive; I will die here!" He clutches at last, above the bed, a gun. "Saved, saved!" He holds it tenderly, as if a child, or something dearly loved. He takes it to the light and looks at the lock; he blows in the barrel; he mournfully shakes his head. "It is not loaded! Well, no matter; I can but die," and he clubs the gun and prepares for mortal battle.

"Oh, come, Carats," cries Gar Dosson, "let's have a little frolic before the sheriff comes—a kiss, eh? Come, my beauty!"

The rough man has all this time been stealing up, as nearly as he could to the girl, and now throws his arm about her neck.

"Shall I brain him—be a murderer, indeed?"

All the Indian is again aroused, and John Logan seems more terrible, and more determined to save her than to defend his own life.

"Stand back!" shouts the Girl to Dosson. She attempts to throw him off, but his powerful arm is about her neck. "Forty-nine! Help!" but the old man is unconscious. John Logan is about to start from his corner.

"Take that, you brute! and that!" and Stumps whirls his club and thunders against the ribs of the ruffian.

"You devil! you brat! what do you mean?"

Mad with disappointment and pain, he throws the girl from him, and turns upon the boy. He clutches him by the back of the neck as he starts to escape, and bears him to the ground.

"Look 'ere, do you know what I 'm going to do with you? I 'm going to break your back across my knee! yes, I am!" and he glares about terribly.

Carrie shrinks back to the side of Forty-nine.

"Oh! Help! He will murder him! He will kill him!"

"No, I won't murder you, you brat, but I'll chuck you out in that snow and let you cool off, while I have your sister all to myself. Come here; give me your ear!" and the great, strong ruffian seizes his ear and fairly carries him along by it toward the door. "Give me your ear!"

"Oh, sister, sister! He will kill me!" howls Stumps.

"Forty-nine! save us! We will be murdered!"

"Come, I say, give me your ear!" thunders the brute, as he fairly draws the boy still toward the door.

"Stop that, or die!"

The frenzied girl, failing to arouse Forty-nine, has caught up the gun from the corner, and brought the muzzle to the ruffian's breast. He totters back, and throws up his arms.

"Go back there and sit down, or I will kill you!"

"Give me your ear! Come!" roars Stumps. It is now his turn. "Give me your ear!" He reaches up and takes that red organ in his hand, and nearly wrenches it from the brute's head, as he leads him back, with many twists and gyrations, slowly to a low seat at the other side of the cabin.

Still holding the gun in level, and in dangerous proximity to the man's breast, Carrie cries:

"Now if you attempt to move you are a dead man!" "Give me your ear!" and Stumps wrenches it again, as he sits the man firmly on his low stool, with his red face making mad distortions from the pain. "John Logan, come!" calls the girl. "No, don 't you start, Gar Dosson. Don 't you lift a finger; if you do, you die!"

The curtains are parted, and John Logan starts forth. "Go, go! There's not a moment to lose. The sheriff will be here; they are coming! Quick! Go at once! I hear—I hear them coming!"

The man springs to the door; the latch is lifted; a moment more and he will be free—safe, at least for the night. Out into the friendly darkness, where man and beast, where pursuer and pursued, are equal, and equally helpless.

There is a crushing of snow, a stamping of feet, and one, two, three, four, five—five forms hurriedly pass the window. The latch is lifted, and as John Logan again darts back under cover, the party, brushing the snow from their coats and grizzled beards, hastily enter the cabin.

"Fly around, Carrie, fly around! fix yourself up!" The fresh gust of wind and storm from the door just opened, fans the glimmering spark of consciousness into sudden flame, and Forty-nine springs up, perfectly erect, perfectly dignified. "Fly around, Carrie, fly around; fix yourself up. The sheriff is coming—fly around!"

The girl drops the gun in the corner where she had found it, and stands before Forty-nine, smoothing down her apron, and letting her eyes fall on the floor timidly and in a childlike way, as if these little hands of hers had never known a harder task than their present employment of smoothing down her apron.

Dosson springs up before the sheriff. He rubs his eyes, and he looks about as if he had just been startled from some bad, ugly dream. He wonders, indeed, if he has seen John Logan at all. Again he rubs his eyes, and then, looking at his knuckle, says, in a deep, guttural fashion, to himself, "Jim-jams, by gol! I thought I'd seed John Logan!"

"Ah, Forty-nine," says the sheriff, "sorry to disturb you, and your Miss; and good evening to you, sir; and good evening to you;"

and the honest sheriff bows to each, and brushes the snow from his fur cap as he speaks.

Gar Dosson advances to his partner, Phin Emens, who has just entered, with that stealthy old tiger-step so familiar to them both, and laying his hand on his shoulder, they move aside.

"Then it's not the jim-jams," mutters he. "I've not got 'em, then."

He stops, pinches himself, looks at his hands, and mutters to himself. Then he lifts his hand to his ear.

"Look at it again!" Phin Emens looks at the ear. "It 's red, ain't it? Oh, it feels red; it feels like fire. Then I 've not got 'em, and he is here. Hist! Come here! We want that thousand dollars all to ourselves."

He plucks his companion further to one side. They talk and gesticulate together, while now and then a big red rough hand is thrust out savagely toward the curtain.

"Sorry indeed to disturb you, Miss," observes the sheriff; "but you see, I 've been searching and swearing of 'em all, and its only fair to serve all alike."

"He is not here. Upon the honor of a

gentleman, he is not here," says Forty-nine, emphatically.

"He is here!" howls Dosson; and the tremendous man, with the tremendous voice and tremendous manner, bolts up before the sheriff. "He is here; and I, as an honest man am going to earn a thousand dollars, for the sake of justice. I have found him—found him all by myself; and these fellers can't have no hand in my find." And he holds up John Logan's cap, which had been knocked from his head in his hasty retreat to cover, and he rolls his red eyes toward the bed, takes a step in that direction, reaches a hand, lays hold of the curtain, and is about to dash it aside.

"John Logan is there!" shouts Dosson, and again the curtain is clutched.

Does he dream of what is beyond? If he could only see the panting, breathless wretch that leans there eagerly, with lifted gun, ready to brain him—waiting, waiting for him to come, even wishing that he only would come—he would start back with terror to the other side.

"He is here! I have found him! Come!"

Carrie, springing forward from her posture of anxiety and terror, grasps a powder horn from over the mantel piece, jerks out the stopple with her teeth, and holding it over the fire, cries, with desperation:

"Do it, if you dare! This horn is full of powder, and if any man here dares to move that curtain, I'll blow you all into burning hell!" The man loosens his hold on the curtain, and totters back. He is sober enough to know how terrible is the situation, and he knows her well enough to believe she will do precisely what she says she will do. "Yes, I will! We will all go to the next world together; and now let us see who is best ready to die!"

"Bravo!" shouts Forty-nine.

The sheriff and his men have been moving back slowly from the inspired girl, standing there by the door of death.

Gar Dosson at last steals around by the sheriff. "But he is here, Mr. Sheriff," he says. "I tell you he is here in this house. There! For here is his cap. I found it. I found him, and I want him and I want that thousand dollars. Search!"

"And I tell you he is not here!" cries the girl, "and you shall not search, 'less—"

And the horn is lifted menacingly over the fire. "Won't you take my word?"

"You shall take *my* word!" shouts Dosson.

"I will take your single word, Miss, against a thousand such men."

And the sheriff puts on his cap, turns, and is about to go.

"But he is here! The thousand dollars, Mr. Sheriff!" cries Dosson.

"Miss, officers sometimes have duties that are more unpleasant to them than to the parties most concerned. You say he is not here?"

"He is not here, Mr. Sheriff—he is not here!" cries Carrie.

The sheriff twists his cap on his head. "And you will be sworn, as the others were?" says the sheriff. "So much the better; and that will be quite satisfactory. Ah, here is the Bible at hand."

And he takes from the little shelf the tattered book. The girl stands still as stone, with the engine of death in her hand. The officer bows, smiles, reaches the book with his left hand, lays his cap on the table, and lifts his right hand in the air. Her little fingers reach out firmly, fearlessly, and rest on the book. Her eyes are looking straight into his.

"It may be my duty, Miss, to search the house, after what that 'un has said, and, Miss, I expect it is my duty. But, Miss, I is not the man to expose you before a man as might like to see you exposed. And then that poor devil that come back here, Miss, on bleeding feet—crawling back here on his hands and knees, to die by his mother's grave."

The voice is tremulous; the hand that is raised in the air comes down. Then lifting it again he says resolutely, "Swear, Miss!"

All are looking—leaning—with the profoundest interest. There is a dark strange face peering through a rift in the half-opened curtain. "God bless her! God bless her! She can, and she will!" mutters Forty-nine.

"She can't!" cries Dosson. "She believes the book and, by gol, she can't!" The man says this over his shoulder, and in a husky whisper as the girl seems to pause.

"Hold your hand on the book, and swear as I shall tell you," says the sheriff.

She only holds more firmly to the book; her eyes are fixed more steadily on his.

"Say it as I say it. I do solemnly swear—"

"I do solemnly swear—"

"That John Logan—"

"That John Logan—"

"Is not here."

"Is—"

"Is *here!*" The curtain is thrown back, and the fugitive dashes into their midst. The book falls from the sheriff's hand, and there is a murmur of amazement.

"God bless you, my girl!" And there is the stillness of a Sabbath morning over all. "God bless you; and God will reward you for this, for I cannot. You have made me another being, Carrie. I have lost my life, but you have saved my soul!" and turning cheerfully to the sheriff he reaches his hands. "Now, sir, I am ready."

CHAPTER VI.

THE ESCAPE.

O tranquil moon! O pitying moon!
Put forth thy cool, protecting palms,
And cool their eyes with cooling alms,
Against the burning tears of noon.

O saintly, noiseless-footed nun!
O sad-browed patient mother, keep
Thy homeless children while they sleep,
And kiss them, weeping, every one.

AT first there was a loud demonstration against Logan by the mob, that always gathers about where a man is captured by his fellows —the wolves that come up when the wounded buffalo falls. There was talk of a vigilance committee and of lynching.

But when the stout, resolute sheriff led the man in chains down the trail through the deep snow, and turned him over to the officer in charge of a little squad of soldiers at the other side of the valley, no man interfered further. Indeed, Dosson and Emens were too anxious about the promised reward to make any demonstration against this man's life now. He was worth to them a thousand dollars.

A lawyer reading this, will smile here at the loose way in which the law was administered there in the outer edge of the world at that time. Here is a sheriff, with a warrant in his pocket, made returnable to a magistrate. The sheriff arrests the man on this warrant and takes him directly to the military authorities, which have been so long seeking him, utterly unconscious that he is doing aught but the proper thing. And yet, after all, it was the shortest and best course to take.

I shall not forget the face of the prisoner as we stood beside the trail in the snow, while he was led past down the mouth of the canyon toward the other side of the valley. It was grand!

Some strangers, standing in the street, spoke of the majesty of the man's bearing. They openly dared to admire his lifted face, and to speak with derision of his captors as the party passed on. This made the low element, out of which mobs are always created, a little bit timid. Possibly it was this that saved the prisoner. But most likely it was the resolute face of the honest sheriff. For, say what you will, there is nothing so cowardly as a mob. Throw what romance you please over the actions of the Vigilantes of California, they were murderers—coarse, cowardly and brutal; murderers, legally and morally, every one of them. It is to be admitted that they did good work at first. But their example, followed even down to this day, has been fruitful of the darkest crimes.

When Forty-nine awoke next morning from his long drunken slumber, the children were not there. Dosson called, arrayed in his best; but Carrie was not to be seen. Forty-nine could give no account of her. This day of triumph for Dosson did not yield him so much as he had all the night before fancied. He was furious.

Forty-nine, as usual, after a spree, meekly took up his pick, after a breakfast on a piece of bread and the drawings of coffee grounds that had been thrice boiled over, and stumbled away towards his tunnel, and was soon lost in the deeps of the earth.

You may be certain that this desperate character, just taken after so much trouble and cost, was securely ironed at the little military camp across the valley. An old log cabin was made a temporary prison, and soldiers strode up and down on the four sides of it day and night.

And yet there was hardly need of such heavy irons. True, the soldiers outside, as they walked up and down at night and shifted their muskets from side to side, and slapped their shoulders with their arms and hands to keep from freezing, heard the chains grate and toss and rattle, often and often, as if some one was trying to tear and loosen them. But it was only the man tossing his arms in delirium as he lay on the fir boughs in the corner.

Dosson, after much inquiry, and many day's watching about Forty-nine's cabin, called and was admitted to see the prisoner, who by this time, though weak and worn to a skeleton, was convalescing. The coarse and insolent intruder started back with dismay. There sat the girl he so hoped and longed to possess, talking to him tenderly, soothing him, giving her life for his.

Long and brutal would be the story of the agent's endeavors to tear this girl away from the bedside of the sufferer—if such a place could be called a bedside. The girl would not leave John Logan, and the timid boy who sat shivering back in the corner of the cabin, would not leave the girl. The three were bound together by a chain stronger than that which bound the wrists of the prisoner; aye, ten thousand times stronger, for man had fashioned the one—God the other.

Sudden and swift arrives summer in California. The trail was opened to the Reservation down the mountain, and the officer collected his few Indians together in a long, single line, all chained to a long heavy cable, and prepared to march. About the middle of the chain stood John Logan, now strong enough to walk. At the front were placed a few miserable, spiritless Indians, who had been found loafing about the miners's cabins—the drunkards, thieves, vagabonds of their tribe, such as all tribes have, such as we have, citizen-reader—

while the rear was brought up by a boy and girl, Carrie and Johnny, a pitiful sight!

Do not be surprised. When you have learned to know the absolute, the utterly unlimited power and authority of an Indian Agent or sub-Agent, you have only to ask the capability for villainy he may possess in order to find the limit of his actions.

Could you have seen the lofty disdain of this girl for her suitor at that first and every subsequent meeting, as she kept at the bedside of John Logan, you could have guessed what might follow. The man's love was turned to rage. He resolved to send her back to the Reservation also. It is true, the soldiers had learned to respect and to pity her. It is true, the little Lieutenant said, with a soldierly oath, as she was being chained, that she was whiter than the man who was having it done. Yet the soldiers, and their officer as well, had their orders; and a soldier's duties, as you know, are all bound up in one word.

As for the wretched boy, he might have escaped. He was a negative sort of a being at best; and no one, save Logan and the girl, either hated him or loved him greatly, tender and true as he was. They both implored him to slip between the fingers of the soldiers and not go to the Reservation. But he would not think of being separated from his sister. Poor, stunted, starved little thing! There were wrinkles about his face; his hands were black, short, and hard, from digging roots from the frosty ground. It is not probable the lad had ever had enough to eat since he could remember. And so he was a dwarf, a dwarf in body and in soul; and instead of showing some spirit and standing up now and helping the girl, as he should, he leaned on her utterly, and left her to be the man of the two. The little spark of fire that had twice or thrice flashed up in the last few years, seemed now to die out entirely, and he stood there chained, looking back now and then over his shoulder at the soldiers, looking forward trying to catch a glance from his sister now and then, but never once making any murmur or complaint.

It was a hot, sultry day, such as suddenly enters and takes possession of canyons in the Sierras, when the little party of prisoners were marched through the little camp at the end of the canyon on their way to the Reservation.

And the camp all came out to see, but the camp was silent. It was not a pleasant sight. A soldier with a bayonet on his loaded musket walking by the side of a woman with her hands in chains, is not an inspiring spectacle. With all respect for your superior judgments, Mr. President, Commander-in-Chief, and Captains of the army, I say there is a nobler use for the army than this.

Let us hasten on from this subject and this scene. But do not imagine that the miner, the settler, or even the most hardened about the camp, felt ennobled at this sight. I tell you there was a murmur of indignation and disgust heard all up and down the cañyon. The newer and better element of the camp was furious. One man even went so far as to write a letter to a country paper on the subject.

But when the editor responded in a heavy leader, and assured the camp of its deadly peril from these prowling savages, and proclaimed that the Indians were being taken where they would have good medicine, care, food and clothing, and be educated and taught the arts of agriculture, the case really did not look so bad ; and in less than a week the whole affair had been forgotten by all the camp. Aye, all, save old Forty-nine.

By the express order of sub-Agent Dosson, the old man, who had been declared a dangerous character by him, was not permitted to see the girl from the first day he discovered that she still clung to Logan. But the old man had worked on and waited. He had kept constantly sober. He would see and would save this girl at all hazards.

And now, as the sorrowful remnant of a once great tribe was being taken, like Israel into captivity, he rushed forward to meet her, to hold her hands, to press her to his heart, and bid her be strong and hopeful.

The agent saw the old man and shouted to the officer ; the officer called to the soldiers—the line moved forward, the bayonets crossed the old man's breast as the prisoners passed on down the mountain, and he saw the sad, pitiful face no more.

Keep the picture before you : Chained together in long lines, marched always on foot in single file, under the stars and stripes, officers in uniforms, clanking swords—the uniform of the Union, riding bravely along the lines! The two men who had done so much to get this desperate Indian out of the way, remained behind to keep possession of his house and land. They had not even the decency to build a new cabin. They only broke down the door, put up a new one with stouter hinges and latch; and the long-coveted land was theirs.

As for old Forty-nine, all the light had left the mountain and the valley now. Carrie, whom he had cared for from the first almost, little Stumps, whom he had found with her, hardly big enough to toddle about—both were gone. All three gone. John Logan, whom he had taught to read and taught a thousand things at his own cabin-fire in the long snowy winters—all these gone together. It was as if the sun had gone down for Forty-nine forever. There was no sun or moon or stars, or any thing that shines in the mountains any more for him. His had been a desolate life all the long years he had delved away into the mountain at his tunnel. No man had taken his hand in friendship for many and many a year.

The man now nailed up his cabin door—an

idle task, perhaps, for men instinctively avoided it, and the trail of late took a cut across the spur of the hill rather than pass by his door. But somehow the old man felt that he might not be back soon. And as men had kept away from that cabin while he was there, he did not feel that they should enter it in his absence.

One evening in the hot, sultry summer, old Forty-nine rode down from the mountain into the great valley, following the trail taken by the lines of chained captives, and set his face for the Reservation.

At a risk of repetition, let us look at this Reservation. The government had ordered a United States officer, of the rank of lieutenant, to set apart a Reservation for the Indians on land not acquired and not likely to be desired by the white settlers, and to gather the Indians together there and keep them there by force, if force should be required. This young man established a Reservation on the border of a tule lake, shut in by a crescent of low sage-brush hills. The Indian camp was laid out on the very edge of this alkali lake. The crescent of sage-brush hills of a mile in circuit, reaching back and almost around the Reservation, was mounted at three points by cannon, ready to sweep the camp below. On this circuit of hills, healthy and pleasant enough the officers and soldiers had their quarters. Down in the damp, deadly valley, on the edge of the alkali lake, the newly appointed Indian Agent, with a tremendous appropriation to be expended in building houses and establishing the Indians in their new homes, built the village. It was made up of two rows of low, one-story, one-room huts. Two big lamps hung in the one street; and from lamp to lamp before the doors of the little huts with earthen floors and turf-covered roofs, paced soldiers night and day.

These houses were damp and dismal from the first. Soon they began to be mouldy; fungi and toadstools and the like began to grow up in the corners and out of the logs. Little shiny reptiles, in the long hot rainy days that followed, and worms and all sorts of hideous vermin, began to creep and crawl through these dreadful dens of death, over the sick and dying Indians. Long slimy, unnamed, and unknown worms crawled up out of the earth, as if they could not wait for the victims to die.

The Indians were dying off by hundreds. They went to the officers and complained. The officers ordered a double guard to be set. And that was all.

You marvel that these young lieutenants could be so imperious and cruel? It does seem past belief. But pardon just one paragraph of digression while we recall the conduct of a younger class only last year on the Hudson. To me the real question before the courts in the Whitaker case is not whether this quiet stranger, with a tinge of black man's blood in his veins, mutilated himself, or no. But the real question is, did they or did they not, by their determined and persistent persecutions and insults, drive him in a fit of desperation to do this in the hope of pulling down ruin on the heads of all? This seems probable to me, and to me is far more monstrous than if they had, in sudden anger, cut his ears, or even cut his throat; and if these young bloods could so treat a stranger there, standing at such a manifest disadvantage, what would they not be capable of when they are, for the first time, clothed with a little brief authority, away out on the savage edge of the world?

The water here, as the hot season came on, was something dreadful. It was slimy with alkali. Little black worms knotted and twisted themselves together at the bottom of the cup, like bunches of witch-woven horse-hair. The Indians were dying of malaria. They were burning up with the fever. And this was the only water these people, who had been used to the fresh sweet snow-water of the Sierras, could have.

What could they do? They appealed to the officers. They were answered with insult: "You must get used to it. You must get civilized."

These dying Indians began to fight and quarrel among themselves. Ah, they were very wicked. They were quarrelsome as dogs; almost as quarrelsome as Christians!

This was a small Paris in siege. It was Jerusalem surrounded by Titus. Down there, dying as they were, a savage Simon and a degenerate John, as in Jerusalem of old, led their followers against each other, even across their dead that lay unburied in the mouldy death-pens and about their dark and narrow doors, and slew each other as did God's chosen people when beseiged by the son of Vespasian.

Then the men in brass and blue turned the cannon loose on the howling savages, and shot them into silence and submission.

John Logan, Carrie and little Stumps, about this time had been brought with others from the mountains to the Reservation. Logan insisted on keeping the two children at his side and under his protection. He was laughed at by agents, and sub-agents.

He was kept chained. He was assigned to a strong hut with gratings across the window—or rather the little loop-hole which let in the light. The guards were kept constantly at his door. He was entered on the books as a very desperate character, a barn-burner, and possible murderer. And so night and day he was kept under the constant watch of the soldiers with fixed bayonets. True, he was soon too weak to lift his manacled hands in strife. But nevertheless he was kept chained and doubly guarded in the little hut with gratings at the loop-hole.

Would he attempt to escape?

There were many broken fragments of many broken tribes here. Tribes that had fought each other to the death—fought as Germans and French have fought. And why not, pray? Has not a heathen as good a right to fight a heathen as has a Christian to fight a Christian? The only difference is, we preach and profess peace; they, war.

Logan was alone in this damp hut and deadly pen. He could hear the tramp of the soldiers; he could see the long thin silver beams of the moon reach through the gratings, reach on and on, around and over and across the damp, mouldy floor, as if reaching out, like God's white fingers, to touch his face, to cool his fever, and comfort him. But he could see, hear nothing more. He was so utterly alone! They would send an unfriendly Indian in with his breakfast, foul and unfit for even a well man, and a tin cup of water in the morning. Soon after the doctor would call around, also. Then he would see no face again till evening, when more food and water would be brought. At last the food was brought only in the morning. This did not at all affect Logan; for from the first the old pan containing his food had been taken away untouched. The man was certainly dying. The guard and garrison on the hill were waiting for this desperate character, whose capture had cost so much time and money, to attempt to escape.

From the first, even in the face of the blunt refusal, John Logan had begged for the boy to be brought him. He was certain the little fellow was dying—dying of desolation and a broken heart.

About the sixth day, the man chanced to hear from an Indian that the boy had quite broken down, and, refusing all food, lay moaning in his corner all the time, and all the time crying for John Logan or Carrie. The man now entreated more persistently than ever before. He promised the Doctor to eat, to get well, if only the boy could be brought to him and be permitted to spend his time there. For he knew from what the Doctor said that he must soon die if things kept on as they were. The weather was growing hotter and hotter; the water and the food, if possible, more repulsive than ever. Logan could no longer walk across the pen in which he was confined. He was so weak that he could not raise his heavily manacled hands to his face.

After the usual diplomacy and delay, the Doctor reported his condition, and also his earnest desire for the boy, to the Indian Agent.

There was a consultation. Would this crafty and desperate Indian attempt to escape? Was not all this a ruse on his part? Would not the United States imperil its peace and security if this boy and this man were to be allowed together? This mighty question oppressed the mind of the agent in charge for a whole day. Then, after the Doctor again urged the prisoner's request—for man and boy both seemed to be dying—this man reluctantly consented. Would Logan now escape after all? Could he ever get through these iron bars and past the four soldiers pacing up and down outside? Would he escape from the Reservation at last?

And now, at the close of the hottest and most dreadful day they had endured, an old Indian woman, bent almost double, came shuffling in by permission of the guard, and laid something on a pile of rushes and willows in a corner of the pen across from where John Logan lay.

The man heard a noise as of some one breathing heavily, and attempted to rise. He could hardly move his head. But in trying to support himself to a sitting posture, he moved his hands, and so rattled his manacles. This frightened the superstitious old woman, and she ran away. She had laid a little skeleton on the rushes in the corner.

Logan with great effort managed to sit up and look across into the corner that was now being slowly illuminated by a beam of bright, white moonlight, that stole down the wall toward the little heap lying there, like some holy, white-hooded and noiseless-footed nun. At last he saw the face. It was that of little Stumps. The man sank back where he lay, The sight was so pitiful, so dreadful to see, that he forgot his own misery and was all in tears for the little fellow who lay dying before him. He forgot his own fearful condition at the sight, and again attempted to rise and reach the little heap that lay moaning in the corner. It was impossible ; he could not rise.

And how fared Carrie all this time? Little better than the others. She was no longer beautiful. And so she was left, along with a score or more of other dying and desperate creatures, in another part of the Reservation. She was not permitted to see the boy. Least of all was she permitted to see, or even hear from, John Logan. Day by day she drooped and sank slowly but surely down toward the grave.

But she did not fear death. She had faced it in all forms before. And even now death walked the place night and day, and she was not afraid. She lay down at night with death. She knew no fear at all. She constantly asked for and wanted to see the helpless little boy, in the hope that she might help or cheer him. But no one listened to anything she had to say. Once, after a very hot and horrible day, two of her companions in captivity were found to be dead. The guard who paced up and down between the huts was told of it. But he said it was too late to have them carted away that night. And so this girl lay there all night by the side of the dead, and was not afraid. Nay, she even wished that she too, when the cart came in the morning, might be found silent and at peace. And then she thought of those whom she loved, and reproached herself for being so selfish as to want to die when she still might be of use to them.

Let us escape from these dreadful scenes as soon as possible. They are like a nightmare to me.

And yet the mind turns back constantly to John Logan lying there; the little heap of bones in the corner; the pure white moonlight creeping softly down the wall, as if to look into the little fellow's eyes, yet as if half afraid of wakening him.

Could Logan escape? Chains, double guards, death—all these at his door holding him back, waiting to take him if he ever passed out at that door. Mould on the floor, mould on the walls, mould on the very blankets. The man was burning to death with the fever; the boy, too, lying over there. The boy moaned now and then. Once Logan heard him cry for water. That warm, slimy, wormy water! O, for one, just one draught of cool, sweet water from the mountains—their dearly loved native mountains—and die!

The moon rose higher still, round and white and large; and at last, wheeling over the camp of death, seemed to pause in pity and look full in upon those two dying captives. It seemed to soothe them both.

The little boy saw the moonbeam on the wall, and was pacified. It looked like the face of an old friend. It brought back the old time; the life, the woods, the water—above all, the cool sweet waters of the mountains. He seemed to know where he was. He lay still a long time, and then felt stronger. He called to John Logan. No answer. Then the feeble, piping little voice lifted up and called as loud as it could. No answer still. The boy crawled from off the little pallet and tried to rise. He sank down on the damp floor, and then tried to crawl to John Logan. He tried to call again, as he began to slowly crawl towards the other corner. But the poor little voice was no louder than a whisper. Very weak and very wild, and almost quite delirious, the boy kept on as best he could. He at last touched the blankets, the breast, and he drew himself up just as the moon looked down on the pale upturned face. Then, with a moan, a wild, pitiful cry, the little fellow fell back on the damp mouldy floor.

John Logan was dead! Despite the chains,

the bars at the window, the double guard at the door, the man had escaped at last!

The pitying moon did not hasten to go. It lingered there, reached down along the damp, mouldy floor to a little form of skin and bone; and then, as if this moon-beam were the Savior's mantle spreading out to cover the white and stainless soul, it covered the pinched and pitiful little face. For the boy, too, lay dead.

Here was the end of two lives that had known only the long dark shadows, only the deep solitude and solemnity of the forest. Like tall weeds that sometimes shoot up in dark and unfrequented places, and that put forth strange, sweet flowers, these two lives had sprung up there, put forth after their fashion the best that is in man, and then perished in darkness, unnamed, unknown.

Who were they? John Logan, it is now whispered, was the son of an officer made famous in the war annals of the world. The officer had been stationed here in early manhood, gave his heart as she believed to a daughter of a brave and powerful chief, whose lands lay near where he was stationed for a summer, and then? The old, old tale of betrayal and desertion. The woman was disgraced before her people. And so when they retreated before the encroachments of the whites, she, being despised and cast off by her people, remained behind waiting the promised return of her lover. He? He did not even acknowledge his child. This General, who had taken the lives of a thousand men, had not the moral courage to reach out a hand to this one little waif which he had called into existence.

Do you know, there never was a dog drowned in the pound so base and low that he would not fight? Yet this brute-valor is largely admired, even to this day, by Christian people. This man could kill men, could risk his own life, but he could not give this innocent child his name.

And so it was, the boy, after he had learned to read, by the help of Forty-nine, and an occasional missionary who sometimes preached to the miners, and spent the pleasant summer months in the mountains—this boy, I say, who at last had heard all the story of his father's weakness and wickedness from Forty-nine's lips disdained to use his name, but chose one famous in the annals of the Indians. And this brief sketch is about all there is to tell of the young man who lay dead in chains, in the prison-pen of the Reservation.

"Civilization kills the Indian," said the Doctor that morning in his daily round, after he had examined the dead bodies.

"He does not look so desperate, after all," said an officer, as he held his nose with his thumb and finger, and leaned forward to look at the dead Indian, while his other hand held his sword gracefully at his side. And then this officer, after making certain that this desperate character was quite dead, drew forth his cigar-case, struck a light, and climbing upon his horse, galloped back to his quarters on the hill.

The Doctor, now left alone, stooped and put back the long silken hair from the thin baby-face of the boy, as the body was brought out and being carried to the cart made to receive the dead, and remarked that it was not at all like that of the other Indians. Another young officer came by as the Doctor did this, and his attention was called to the fact. The officer tapped his sword-hilt a little, looked curiously at the pitiful, pinched little face, and then ordering the soldiers to move on with their burden, he turned to the Doctor and remarked, as the two went back together to their quarters on the hill, that "no doubt it was the effect of the few days of civilization on the Reservation that had made the boy so white; pity he had died so soon; a year on the Reservation, and he would have been quite white."

Unlike other parts of the Union, here the races are much mixed. Creoles, Kanakas, Mexicans, Malays, whites, and blacks, have intermixed with the natives, till the color line is not clearly drawn. And in one case at least some orphan children of white parentage were sent to the Reservation by parties who wanted their property. Though I do not know that the fact of white children being found on a Reservation makes the sufferings of the savages less or their wrongs more outrageous. I only mention it as a frozen fact.

Carrie did not know of the desolation which death had made in her life, till old Forty-nine, who arrived too late to attend the burial of his dead, told her. She did not weep. She did not even answer. She only turned her face to the wall as she lay in her wretched bed, burning up with the fever, but made no sign. There was nothing more for her to bear. She had felt all that human nature can feel. She was dull, dazed, indifferent, now to all that might occur.

To turn back for the space of a paragraph, I am bound to admit that these dying Indians often behaved very foolishly, and, in their superstitions brought much of the fatality upon themselves. For example, they had a horror of the white man's remedies, and refused to take the medicines administered to them. Brought down from the cool, fresh mountains, where they lived under the trees in the purest air and in the most beautiful places, they at once fell ready victims to malarial fevers. The white man, by a liberal use of quinine and whisky, as well as by careful diet, lived very well at the Reservation, and suffered but little, yet had he been forced to live in a pen, crowded together like pigs in a sty, with the bad air, on the damp, mouldy ground, he had died too, as fast perhaps as the Indian died.

The old man could do but little for the

dying girl. He was in bad odor with the officers; they treated him with as little consideration almost as if he too had been a savage. But he was constant at her side; he brought a lemon which he had begged, on his knees, as it were, and tried to make her a cool drink of the slimy, wormy water. But the girl could not drink it. She turned her face once more to the wall, and this time, it seemed, to die.

One morning, before the sun rose, she recovered her wandering mind and called old Forty-nine to her side. She was surely dying; but her mind was clear, and she understood perfectly all she said or did. Her dark eyes were sunken deep in their places, and her long, sun-browned hands were only skin and bone. They fell down across her heaving little breast, as if they were the hands of a skeleton. Little wonder that her persecutors had turned away with horror, perhaps with fear, from those deep, hollow eyes, and the pitiful emaciated frame, that could no longer lift itself where it lay.

The old man fell down on his knees beside

her and reached his face across to hers. With great effort she lifted her two naked long, arms, and wound them about the old man's neck. He seemed to know that death was near, as he reached his face over hers. Over his cheeks and down his long white beard the tears ran like rain and fell on her face and breast.

"Forty-nine, father! Let me call you father; may I? I never had any father but you," said the girl feebly, as the tears fell fast on her face.

"Yes, yes, call me father. Call me father, Carrie, my Carrie; my poor, dear, dear little Carrie,—do call me father, for of all the world I have only you to love and live for," sobbed the old man as if his heart would break.

"Well, then, father, when I die take me back, take me back to the mountains. I want to hear the water—the cool, sweet, clear water, where I lie; and the wind in the trees—the cool, pure wind in the trees, father. And you know the three trees just above the old cabin on the hill by the water-fall? Bury me, bury me there. Yes, there, where I can hear the cool water all the time, and the wind in the trees. And—and won't you please cut my name on the tree by the water? My name, Carrie—just Carrie, that 's all. I have no other name—just Carrie. Will you? Will you do this for me?"

"As there is a God—as I live, I will!" and the old man lifted his face as he bared his head, and looked toward heaven.

The girl's mind wandered now. She spoke incoherently for a few moments, and then was silent. Her form was convulsed, her breast heaved just a little, her helpless hands reached about the old man's neck as if they would hold him from passing from her presence; they fell away, and then all was still. It was now gray dawn.

This man's heart was bursting with rage and a savage sorrow. He was now stung with a sense of awful injustice. His heart was swelling with indignation. He took up the form before him; up in his arms, as if it had been that of an infant. He threw his handkerchief across the face as he passed out, stooping low through the dark and narrow doorway, and strode in great, long and hurried steps down the street and over toward the hills beyond, where his horse was tethered in the long, brown grass.

As the old man passed the post on the hill, where the officers slept under the protection of loaded cannon, the guard stopped him with his bayonet.

"Halt! Where are you going? And what have you there? Come, where are you going?

The old man threw back the handkerchief as the guard approached, and the new sunlight fell on the girl's face.

"I am going to bury my dead."

The guard started back. He almost dropped his gun as he saw that face; then, recovering himself, he bared his head, bowed his face reverently, and motioned the old man on.

Forty-nine reached his horse in the brown grass, laid his burden down, threw on the saddle, drew the girth with sudden strength and energy, as if for a long and desperate ride. Then resuming his load, tenderly, as if it were a sleeping infant, he vaulted into the saddle and dashed away for the Sierras, that lay before him, and lifted like a city of snowy temples, reared to the worship of the Eternal.

It was a desperate ride for life. The girl's

long soft black hair was in the wind. The air was purer, sweeter here; there was a sense of liberty, of life, in this ride, right in the face of the rising sun as it streamed down over the snowy summits of the Sierras. Every plunge of the strong swift, mustang, brought them nearer to home, to hope, to life. The horse seemed to know that now was his day of mighty enterprise. Perhaps he was glad to get away and up and out of that awful valley of death; for he forged ahead as horse never plunged before, with his strange double burthen, that had frightened many a better trained mustang than he.

At last they began to climb the chapparal hills. Then they touched the hills of pine, and the breath of balsam had a sense of health and healing in it that only the invalid who is dying for his mountain home can appreciate.

The horsè was in a foam; the day was hot; the old man was fainting in the saddle.

Water! Water at last! Down a steep, mossy crag, hung with brier and blossom, came tumbling, with loud laughter like merry girls at play, a little mountain stream. Cool as the snow, sweet as the blossom, it fell foaming in its pebbly bed at the base of the crag, under the deep. cool shadows of the pines.

The old man threw himself from his horse, and beast and man drank together as he held the girl in his arms, where the spray dashed down like a holy baptismal from the very hand of God upon her hair and face. The hands clutched, the breast heaved a little, the lips moved as if to drink in the cool sweet water. Her eyes feebly opened. And then the old man bore her back under the pines, and laid her on the soft bed of dry sweet-smelling pine-quills.

Then clasping his hands above her, as he bent his face to hers, he uttered his first prayer—the first for many and many a weary year. It was a prayer of thanksgiving, of gratitude. The girl would live; and he would now have something to live for—to love.

It had been a strange weird sight, that old man, his long hair in the wind, his strong horse plunging madly ahead, all white with foam, climbing the Sierras as the sun climbed up. The girl lay in his arms before him, her long dark hair all down over the horse's neck, tangled in the horse's mane, catching in the brush and the wild vines and leaves that hung over the trail as they flew past.

And oftentime back over his shoulder the old man threw his long white beard and looked back. He felt, he knew, that he was pursued. He fancied he could all the time hear the sound of horses' feet.

Perhaps if his eyes had been gifted with the vision of the prophets of old, he would indeed have seen the pursuer. That pursuer was also an old man, and not much unlike himself; an old man with a scythe—death. Death following fast from the hot valley of pestilence, where he, death, kept, if possible, closer watch than the Agents, that no Indian ever returned to his native mountains. But death gave up the pursuit, and turned back from the moment the baptismal fountain touched the girl's fevered forehead. At last the old man who held her in his arms, rose up, rode on and down to his cabin in the twilight, all secure from pursuit of Agents, death, or any one. The girl, quite conscious, opened her eyes and looked around on the tall, nodding pine trees, that stood in long, dusky lines, as if drawn up to welcome her return to the heart of the Sierras.

"Thoughtful in substance and vigorous and eloquent in style."—
Congregationalist, Boston.

CLUB ESSAYS,

(SECOND EDITION.)

BY PROF. DAVID SWING,

Author of "MOTIVES OF LIFE," and "TRUTHS FOR TO-DAY."

Square 16 mo., ... ***Price, $1.00.***

"Vigorously and charmingly written."—*Christian Advocate, N. Y.*

"Like everything written by Prof. Swing, these essays are graceful in style and full of pleasant thoughts and suggestions."—*Gazette, Cincinnati.*

"For delicate humor, refined and poetic expression, lighted up here and there with a flashing metaphor, they are not readily matched among the productions of essayists."—*The Interior.*

"They are, taken together, the best literary work the professor has yet given to the public. The poetical quality of his mind glows in their genial pages, while their intellectual structure is robust and vigorous." —*Times, Chicago.*

"Prof. Swing's work is a typical product of the West. It is breezy, daring and strong; to a certain extent iconoclastic, yet with an enthusiasm not often met in the quieter writers of the East who might treat of the same subject."—*Press, Philadelphia.*

"As an essayist Professor Swing has few equals and hardly a superior in the entire range of men and letters. With profound scholarship he combines wonderfully keen analytical powers, a terse mode of expression, and a direct style of dealing with his subject. * * * There is a mint of solid gold in these Club Essays."—*Home Journal, Boston.*

Sold by booksellers, or mailed, postpaid, on receipt of price, by

JANSEN, McCLURG & CO., Publishers,

117 and 119 State Street, CHICAGO.

www.ingramcontent.com/pod-product-compliance
Lightning Source LLC
LaVergne TN
LVHW011217110826
845150LV00006B/1455

* 9 7 8 1 4 2 5 5 1 6 4 1 3 *